ESCAPE Reality

A COLLECTION OF SHORT STORIES
EDITED BY FUZZY FLAMINGO

Published by Fuzzy Flamingo
www.fuzzyflamingo.co.uk

ISBN 978-1-9161147-6-0

A CIP catalogue record for this book is available from the British Library

Cover design, typesetting and editing: Fuzzy Flamingo
www.fuzzyflamingo.co.uk

Dedicated to everyone affected by COVID-19

CONTENTS

FOREWORD

Lucy McCarraher

Escaping reality – something we all need to do from time to time, and perhaps especially now while we are living restricted and uncertain lives, having to find new ways to manage practicalities like food, exercise and education; and emotions like anxiety, boredom and frustration.

For me, the joy of both reading and writing fiction has always been that it provides a portal into a parallel universe, a form of mindfulness and meditation, and an insight into other realities great and small. This ability to create new worlds from nothing but the manipulation of words on a page is the ultimate human superpower; it extends the lives of writers and readers, and allows us to understand the experience of others across continents and centuries.

Jen Parker's initiative to create a book of short stories by women for the coronavirus era is a stroke of brilliance.

Twenty-two authors (including Jen) have contributed a banquet of alternative realities for us to dip into for delectable snacks, or devour as a single substantial meal. Here are stories from mature women and youthful creatives (the youngest are eleven and thirteen years old); from first-time fiction-writers, and experienced authors; presented as journaled reality and traditional fiction through to fantasy and magical realism.

Each story is unique, and between them they reflect wide-ranging experiences and viewpoints. I have been intrigued by a number of themes that have emerged from the diversity.

The Coronavirus environment features explicitly only in Leah Strachan's positive and neatly structured 'A Birthday To Remember', but I found echoes of lockdown in Anne Ceesay's cryptic 'It's Not Me, It's You', and perhaps a COVID-19 inspired post-apocalyptic vision from Alex Preston in 'Willow Trees and Rainbows'.

But gardens, particularly as imaginative spaces for children (and currently our saving graces of outside space) feature as settings in several pieces, from Joanne Norwood's charming period piece 'The Great Garden Escape', to Charlotte Ryan's recycling fantasy 'Educating Someone with an Empty Brain'.

Perhaps unsurprisingly, the theme of escape, in a range of guises, runs through many of the short stories in *Escape Reality*. 'This Is Africa' by Zoe Brooks takes us to Africa, but the escape in 'Maggie's Adventure' by Kirsty France is from the ties of a worn-out relationship. In a very different scenario with a frisson of danger throughout, Paris Booton also negotiates us through her apparently naïve heroine's disentanglement from a returning ex-lover.

The protagonist of Laura Bland's 'Oblivion' never entirely reveals to the reader or the police the reason she had to escape from damage and destruction, as she fades in and out of that oblivion. 'Still Here', a short but insightful piece by Paula Robbins, unpacks a personal journey where the main character allows herself to escape from a background and mindset where life feels like a continual battle to one of acceptance and enjoyment.

Jen Parker's tale of magical realism combines the reality of a child in a painfully real situation with a flight of fantasy that could be read as a metaphor or an actual means of escape. 'Boxed In' also links into what is perhaps the most consistent theme throughout the collection of stories – parents, and the power of Mum and Dad. This dad remains a shadowy, cold, perhaps Victorian figure; a harsh and emotionally unavailable parent to a young girl following a mother's disappearance.

Fathers mostly get less than sympathetic treatment in *Escaping Reality*. In 'Call It Off' Laura Lawrence shows us a father whose inflexible views cause at least one of his daughters to hide her truth until she no longer can. And the main character in 'Vanilla', a creepy office worker with predatory thoughts, turns out to be no more than a self-obsessed husband and father having a midlife crisis.

The mothers portrayed in this collection of stories are more warmly depicted, even when they are shown as flawed human beings. Tania Taylor's dark tale 'The Call' leaves us sympathetic to two mothers whose crimes are an almost inevitable response to the cycle of domestic violence. Laura Goodsell tracks an extraordinary year in which the improving relationship with the main character's mother is one of the positive 'Lessons of Life, Love and Fear'.

All of the short stories in *Escaping Reality* are reflective and many draw on 'memories' – perhaps those of the author or the fictional memories of their characters. Louise Stone's 'No Words Required' interrogates the nature of memory through the photographic images we choose to create and store through our lives. Two other authors use the potent metaphor of the mirror to tell their stories: in D. Wells' poignantly articulated 'Reflected', the mirror brings reconciliation and new confidence to an older cancer survivor; and Kate Wells takes a more fantastical approach in 'Reflections' where the mirror is a portal to an alternative life and better choices for her heroine.

Jen has curated the twenty-two stories into an engaging and emotionally varied journey of contrasts and surprises interspersed with moments of calm and humour. For those of us who enjoy a good crime drama, we get Ruby Perry's topical 'Dream Connection' towards the end of the book, where the dangers of online grooming are made disturbingly real; and for a seriously grim and gruesome murder plot, Michelle Chambers brings us 'Masterpieces'.

Bringing us back to light and some laughter, Lauren Raybold's 'A Day in the Life of an Outdoor Cat' enters this collection with a wry look at the unimpressive human characters that populate the life of this particular feline.

Congratulations to all the authors who have contributed to *Escaping Reality*, and to Jen Parker for conceiving, curating and publishing this delightful and timely volume.

Lucy McCarraher
Co-Founder, Rethink Press
Author, *How To Write Fiction Without The Fuss*

IT'S NOT ME; IT'S YOU

Anne Ceesay

I fear for my life. I am surrounded by people with mask-like smiles and concerned brows who, in reality, seek my downfall. They call me 'paranoid' (no, really, I've heard them), but they are the ones stuck in a fog of ignorance. My sight is crystal clear – my mind's eye sees things with 20:20 vision. I see the truth in all its glorious, yet abhorrent, beauty.

I'm safe. For now. From my vantage point on the sofa I see all. The slightly yellowing net curtains and long-neglected windows lend a slightly blurry quality to my view, but that only adds to my camouflage. I still see everything. Am I the hunter or the prey? Who is stalking whom?

The elderly man from next door, for example. He insists on whistling as he walks that scrawny dog of his past my gate. Every damn day! He shuffles along, almost invisible – a crepey, grey ghost in his tired old flat-cap and greasy, creased overcoat – and I could happily ignore him if it wasn't for that aimless, high-pitched piping that comes from his puckered, old lips. It's an assault to my brain – like a dentist's drill hitting a nerve full force. For that reason, and that alone, I hate him.

Don't get me started about the family across the road! They are the perfect 2.4 family with the ubiquitous Volvo on the drive and oversized trampoline in the back garden. They are just as bad. They flaunt their 'togetherness'. The parents actually seem to like each other and the children are well-nourished, polite and well-behaved. Or are they? Their high-pitched squeals of delight jangle my nerves and the repetitive thump… thump… thump of their football against the wall is a suburban sledgehammer to my brain. They do it on purpose – no one enjoys playing with a ball *that* much!

Then there's the garrulous woman on the other side. I've overheard people refer to her as "friendly", "salt-of-the-earth", and "that Jean's got a heart of gold". I call her the "soul sucker". As soon as she starts talking to me in her well-meaning, over-sharing way, I can feel the very life-blood draining from me. My energy gauge plummets to 'empty' and I can feel my eyes darting about in a panic, desperate to find the emergency exit.

Inside my house, however, I am safe. For now. My routines and rituals contain me. They are my fortress. They are the only things that make sense. Inside my world, everything makes sense as long as nothing and nobody disturbs me and there are no changes to the predictable flow of my day. Don't pity me. I'm not lonely. I have my faithful companion. The one who has stayed loyally by my side since childhood. By my side, in my head, my heart and every fibre of my being. I truly don't know who I would be without it. We have this dysfunctional, symbiotic relationship. We've become interchangeable – we blur into one entity. The comfortable familiarity of discomfort; anxiety.

I am fine. We are fine. Just leave us be.

★★★

Anne lives in Leeds with her daughter. This is her first published story. She works with children with additional needs and autism. Anne also has her own Play Therapy practice, which supports children experiencing emotional difficulties and behaviour issues:

www.peacockplaytherapy.co.uk

THE CALL

Tania Taylor

I woke with a start. I can't remember the last time I was woken by my child standing hovering above me as I lay sound asleep in my bed.

It's one of those eery sixth sense moments. One minute you're comfortably sleeping, and the next your heart's just jumped through the ceiling as you open your eyes to a ghostly pale face that's inches away from your own. Relieved, moments later, you realise it was the face of your own flesh and blood, your little girl.

So, here I was, experiencing a time lapse, my heart racing, wondering what on earth my – now teenage – daughter was doing hovering above my bed?

"Mum, are you awake?" she asked.

"What's wrong?" Why did my thoughts go straight to what was wrong? I suppose it was probably due to the fact that it was 4am.

It was 4am and there my daughter stood, with her long teenage legs, wearing her nightgown, telephone in hand.

"Mum, did you not hear the phone ringing? It's

Aunty Donna. She said she needs to speak to you." She handed me the phone.

Donna's voice sounded echoey through the crackling line. "Sarah? Has Martine left the room?"

I shooed Martine back to her bedroom, told her everything was fine and to go to sleep, and awaited the news that was so important I had to be woken at 4am.

To give you an idea of my life up to this point, 4am phone calls were not normal for us. In fact, I don't think I had ever received a call at 4am since I was a teenager.

What was my sister about to tell me? My thoughts raced ten to the dozen. Had someone died? Was someone rushed into hospital? Was she stuck somewhere and needed money?

I sat myself up in my double bed. Now only half of it used since my husband had been called away to work last week. I suddenly felt so alone. Cold even. My arms bristled with goosebumps.

"Martine has left, Donna, what's happened?" I asked again as Donna tried to unmix her words.

I sat in darkness waiting for the words that were about to change my life forever.

"Get to your TV now, Sarah, turn on BBC News," Donna said with an urgency I have never heard in her voice before.

My stomach was lurching with butterflies, my movements slow and lumbered as I adjusted my pyjamas that were skew-whiff from a night spent tossing and turning worrying about Jack, my husband, and what undercover operation he was on right now.

It was always the same when he was away. My nights were sleepless, my days I often found myself daydreaming, wondering what he was up to, hoping he was safe. Conjuring up a million different scenarios of "the knock" on the door. I dreaded the thought of the police or army or MI5, whoever, coming to knock on my door to tell us our lives had been forever changed.

I found myself frantically trying to locate the television remote, simultaneously pleading to my younger sister. "Donna, just tell me!" I practically whined, as though we were back at home with our parents.

"I can't, you can't say this, you need to see it, Sarah!"

"At 4am?!" I let out a huge yawn as I eventually located the remote control down the side of the sofa.

Pressing the power button and waiting for what felt like an eternity.

I was in the midst of making a series of memories leading up to a moment that I would never be allowed to forget.

The TV began showing signs of life. I looked around my living room. Modest as living rooms go. A plush aubergine deep purple carpet and matching curtains surrounded by pale ivory painted walls. The TV was mounted on the wall opposite me. A small wood burner was to the left of the sofa I perched on. The embers now completely grey and ashen after being lit the night before. I yawned again; Donna was becoming impatient with me.

And there it was. I sat awestruck.

No one knows the torture I felt inside at that very moment. The conflicting thoughts. The big decisions that normally would be left to lie for another few days, but I had the urgency to make them right in that moment. There was no time to waste.

How is this even happening? This could have the power to break me. The power to break all of us. Life as we know it… gone, all gone, in an instant.

My mouth was completely dry. I had already started to sweat. My heart was pumping. Pounding in my head. Thumping relentlessly. What was I going to tell the kids?

Should I go and wake them now? Maybe I should let them get their rest?

Should I start packing? We need to get away from here.

"Sarah, have you seen it?" Donna's voice echoed down the crackling line.

I tried to speak but all that came out was a strange croak. None of this made sense. My brain wasn't prepared to process it.

"Yes," I eventually managed in response.

"What are you thinking, Sarah?" Her voice interrupted my thoughts. My thoughts that were still going at a thousand miles per hour.

What was I thinking? What do I think about, about, THIS?

Can I put my thoughts into words right now? No, I needed a moment.

"Err…" I spoke, holding the unasked, unanswered question in the air.

"You're still the oldest, Sarah, I don't know what to do. What should we do? How will we get through this?" she pleaded.

I sat with the phone to my ear, cradling my head and the phone together. The whirr of the tinny voices on BBC News playing on a loop in the room.

I was panicked. Completely panicked. No, worse! I ran to the toilet, dropping the handset on my way, as I felt the bile rising in my mouth. I got to the toilet in the nick of time before last night's tea projected from my mouth.

Tears flooded my face. I coughed and coughed, praying that it would end. That all this would end. Wishing I was in the middle of a nightmare. But no matter what I did, I knew this was real life. I couldn't stop the world from spinning.

After swilling my mouth with water and coughing some more, I eventually got back to the handset I'd left lying on the hallway carpet.

Donna was beside herself in tears. She had heard me retching, but I think the whole thing was just too much for her.

"Pack your things, get Casey and her things too. Tell her it's a holiday and drive straight over to mine. Don't stop for anyone or anything, come straight here. We will tell all our children together." I took control of the situation, just like I always did when disaster struck in our lives.

There was the time Donna had been in an abusive relationship. I knew I had to keep being there for her, even when I didn't feel like being supportive, but I was always there. I guided her, listened to her, gently encouraging her to acknowledge that abuse of any kind was never acceptable. Whether it was mind games or physical. It took longer than I anticipated, but I was there when she needed me to help her.

We had always been close, only two years apart in age but more like best friends or mother and daughter than sisters, really. Mum had died when we were just eleven and nine. Dad wasn't great with two adolescent girls about to hit puberty, so it was up to me to do all the research and make sure Donna was fully informed about what was to be expected when she herself hit puberty too.

I took her to buy her first bra, she came with me to buy mine. We've been inseparable since we had to watch Mum slowly decline over our early years.

Mum had postnatal depression after having both of us, and she never really got past that. We could have wallowed in self-pity at the fact she left us out of choice. She chose to end her life, but we both understood mental health and how soul destroying it could be if you didn't reach out and get support as soon as you started to feel low or anxious.

After saying goodbye to Donna and repeatedly telling her to drive safely but not to stop anywhere, under any costs, I began frantically packing our own things.

I really wanted to call my husband, but I had no way to do it. When he's undercover, he's unreachable and I just have to hope and pray he calls me instead. He will find a way if he sees the news, but what if his current operation doesn't allow him to see the news?

What if he's off in the middle of the Atlantic Ocean on some submarine? Or in the middle of the black sea on some cargo ship? Maybe he's in the middle of the Amazon jungle living off the land.

My head always went a little crazy trying to imagine what he would get up to on these undercover missions. He wasn't allowed to tell me. It was top secret stuff, so I just had to trust that he would be safe and that he would come home.

Gosh, what if he comes home? Should I leave a note? What if someone breaks in when we're gone, do I want them to see a note?

Maybe I could write a coded note. My mind is just as frantic as my packing. How are we going to tell the kids about this?

I needed to sit down for a minute and think things through. Donna was a half hour drive away and she still had to pack and get Casey up and dressed. I had time to sit down with a piece of toast and a hot cup of tea.

I did just that. I purposefully ate my toast mindfully, thinking about how the ingredients for the bread had been made. I wondered which country the flour was farmed in and how many people were involved in getting the ingredients from the ground to being on my plate. It gave me some time to stop for a moment. I drank my tea whilst it was still hot, scalding my tongue and the roof of my mouth a little. I could hear the birds singing their morning birdsong outside.

For them, today was a normal day. Their days would continue to be normal. Meanwhile our life as we know it was never going to be the same again.

By the time Donna called me to say her and Casey were outside, I was dressed and had packed as much as I could for a few days. Martine and Daniel, my own teenage children, were also reluctantly up and dressed, complaining of being tired.

I had already told Donna that I'd changed my mind. "Let's not tell the kids what's happening yet. Let's just up and go. We'll figure it out."

"We're surprising you all!" I said shrilly, hardly hiding my anxious state. "We're going away on a 'back to basics' trip, you'll need to leave your phones at home. No electronic devices at all." I barely finished before complaints came thick and fast.

"But what about Kylie?" Martine whined. Kylie was her girlfriend, they'd been dating a few months now, lovely girl. "Kylie can cope without hearing from you for a few days, tell her we're going on a 'back to basics' trip, you'll call her soon." I was firm, but gentle. Reassuring.

"I'm not going!" Daniel frowned.

"If he's not going, then I'm not going either," Martine quipped.

"You're both coming, you're both leaving your electronics at home, and we're all leaving in five minutes, so get your things together sharpish, we won't be coming home for anything," I ordered, losing my patience. And with that, they continued to grumble, but they were good kids and ten minutes later we were all out of the door and sitting in our Range Rover, Donna and Casey – who was still sleeping – too.

Only ninety minutes had passed since being woken up by Donna's call and now we were off and driving. The roads were quiet. The sun hadn't yet risen. There was an eeriness about the world. Spring was in the air; you could hear it in the birdsong. And we drove, mainly in silence, telling the kids we had no current destination in mind. Donna and I just knew we had to get away from here. Far, far, away.

We drove for hours being careful not to pull up to any service stations. We couldn't afford to be seen on camera anywhere.

The kids complained about having to pee in the bushes, but we just continued with the 'back to basics' game. They knew both Donna and I had been on lots of camping trips in the past. We knew the ropes. We knew how to disappear off the grid, and that's just what we did.

I'd already changed the plates on the Range Rover before we'd set off. I had a full tank of diesel and two more full cans in the boot.

I'd planned for this journey for a long time; hoping this day would never come.

As I drove, my mind played back the most traumatic day of our lives. We were only sixteen and fourteen, Donna and me. It was too young. But we hadn't had a choice.

We had seen the results of abuse on our mum. It wasn't just postnatal depression that drove her away from us. It was Dad's constant daggers. Telling her she wasn't attractive enough, telling her she wouldn't get into college and if she tried to make herself attractive, he'd hit her and accuse her of getting made-up for another man.

Our childhood was not great. We had done our best for our own children, but we had no great childhood to base our own parenting upon.

After Mum died, everything was calm for a short while, but then Dad's attention turned first to me, and then eventually to Donna.

I could cope when it was just me. I had a hard shell. But Donna was more delicate, she needed taking care of.

When Dad turned on Donna, Donna and I turned on Dad. We laced his food with rat poison, weakening him, until eventually he died in his bed.

When Casey's dad had turned out just like ours, we knew what we had to do to allow Donna to leave him behind for good.

I had no regrets; these men were evil. We had been left with nothing, but we had made a good life for ourselves anyway. And we were going to keep having a good life.

After seeing the bodies had been found, though, we knew it was only a matter of time before they would come knocking at our doors. I cursed myself for burying them together. If only they were miles apart, me and Donna wouldn't be the first people the police would come looking for.

A wave of nausea swept over me again.

We could do this. We were doing this. We had prepared for this. Everything was going to be okay.

"Are we nearly there yet" Casey's tiny six-year-old voice came from the back seat.

"Where are we going anyway?" Martine asked.

"Won't be long now," Donna answered. "There's a great campsite. Camp Inglesdon, about thirty minutes' drive. Mummy and Aunty Sarah have been here before, you're all going to love it".

That appeared to satisfy them all and it wasn't long before we were pulling in to Camp Inglesdon.

And there waiting for us was the police. My stomach lurched; my heart began thudding like it was going to burst out of my chest. It was like something from a movie, as one of them shouted over a loudspeaker, "Sarah and Donna get out of the vehicle slowly with your hands above your head."

"What the…?" I exclaimed. How could they know we were coming here?

And out stepped my husband, Jack. It was in that moment my life shattered into tiny pieces. My heart was crushed.

Ten days later.

Martine's words:

Dad had always told me that if ever I was being kidnapped or felt unsafe, I needed to activate this app he'd installed on my phone and make sure I kept my phone with me at all times.

We had both thought it would keep me safe from strangers. Never in my life did I think I'd be activating it because of my own mum! But I knew something wasn't right.

I'd heard the news on the TV when Mum had told me to creep back up to bed.

I knew Mum needed Dad's help, but I didn't know why.

Our lives have been turned upside down, but we're getting through it.

Dad's off undercover operations for good, and he's got an interim care order for Casey.

I asked him how he got there before we did. He'd already guessed from my tracker that that's where we would be headed. Mum had mentioned the place several times before. As for Dad, his undercover operation was in a bank in Scotland, only three hours from where we ended up.

Mum and Aunty Donna are in prison on remand awaiting a hearing. Dad says the evidence is strong and that we need to prepare for a life with our mums in lock-up.

I wonder if I'm to blame. If I hadn't have activated my app, or texted Dad the name of the campsite, would Mum be okay now?

She says she doesn't blame me, but I worry that she always will.

★★★

Tania Taylor is an International Multi-Award-Winning Hypnotherapist and Psychotherapist. A national campaigner for the rights of vulnerable people with #JusticeForGraham, and a two times #1 bestselling author.

She has two children and a loving partner, Adam, and lives in a small village in Lancashire:

www.Tania-Taylor.co.uk

NO WORDS REQUIRED

Louise Stone

I'm sitting awkwardly, crossed-legged on the floor in my warmly lit bedroom, my legs feeling as dead as my soul right now. Warm tears slowly trickle down my flushed cheeks. Laid out in front of me is a lifetime of people I've loved, loved and lost. Whilst others are imposters, those who were once significant to my existence but are no more. Colourful dreams, places that gave me time out from my immediate reality. I sit staring at these old photographs. I hear echoes in my ears of all those sentiments you hear when looking at snapshots from the past. Like 'you've not aged', 'I can't believe how much weight I've put on', 'look at that beautiful smile', 'I wish I was there now', 'I can't believe they're no longer with us'. My precarious life confirmed in print and sealed in certainty. The words spoken that no one can hear any more. Those cherished moments, so captured in time that I can almost hear a heartbeat.

I'm not sure if these tears are happy or sad expressions. I guess it's a confused mixture of the two. My eyes focus sharply on the tattered brown box that created a window to my memory. It's a worn box and at this moment I think it's probably about the same age as me. I gently smile and see the similarities to being a bit worn and tattered around the edges. Some aged stains from a life that's been filled with black and white nightmares with the occasional flashes of colour.

Little did I know when I was gifted this box that it would hold a mechanical time machine. A magnificent machine that has the ability to gift from day one and continue to gift you treasures for an eternity. When I first received this big clunky machine, I was grateful for it had been a gift. Then I thought of all the inconvenience of carrying it around with me. 'I won't take my camera to the beach, it'll get wet, or get sand in it, or someone will probably see an opportunity to steal it from me'. 'I won't take my camera today, it will just get heavily slung over my shoulder, it will rub on my sunburnt neck'. If only I'd have realised that 'not taking my camera today' may be as significant as not having a map for my final destination. I would never have harnessed people, places, fashion, architecture, silly moments and memorable occasions that seemed vitally important to me at that precise moment in time.

I shift a little and stretch out my legs to alleviate a growing sense of pain. A feeling of immense sadness washes over me. These moments I have witnessed today had been lost, over, until now. I can hear an incredible silence and, in another life, I hear laughter. A child laughing. That carefree sound of total oblivion. Laughing at the world with such sweet innocence. Was that me?

I am six or seven and I am playing in the local fields, filthy, hungry and truly not a care in the world. Not yet aware, thankfully, of the twists and turns of life up ahead. Family photographs were surely just awkward moments that I had to endure. I sense I would have wanted to view the negatives first before I agreed to print the life that was going to become my own.

I reach out for one more pile of photographs and settle down with now dried tears on my face. The light's fading and I shiver. I feel that I want this moment to last forever. I had lost these memories once and I didn't want to lose them to time again. I want to hear my father speak, I want to feel the warmth of the sun on my neck, smell the freshness of the sea, feel that strong hand entwined in mine.

I feel as if I have travelled a thousand miles as I sit here. I'm weary. I don't want to pack all these pictures away. They have earned a special place in my history, my family's history. My future generations' history. I am not to be selfish.

I get up and go to the window. It's dusk and I am completely bewildered as to where the last three hours have gone. I feel so thirsty I cannot moisten my lips. I can only taste the faded tears. The street below is quiet and fitting to my mood. I wander over to the heavy oak dressing table and reach for my hairbrush. It feels soothing to brush my long greying hair. In a way it did as a child. I pick up a photograph frame with both hands and clutch the cold metal frame against my bare chest. This person in the picture filled my life with such richness and love. I can hear my chest beating fast as I hold it tighter. I wish for the warmth of their breath as I'm holding them close. To feel their body pressing back against mine. This is the power, the magic, of what that tattered old brown box given to me many years ago can create. A portal to the time and place. Like smelling a sweet perfume or hearing that special song.

I have no fear of what's to come. I have lived an incredible life with the most amazing people. I have travelled to some wonderful places known on earth. It no longer matters that life has been cruel, that I have regrets, that I have suffered unbearable pain. I have my memories. And when these memories fade, as they are doing much more often now, I will sit and look, and reminisce. A window to my memories will continue thanks to that gift I received all those years ago. A timeless, futuristic time machine that gives you back moments of your life that were important to you. I hope my children, and their children and my children's children, see what I see, through my eyes in the click of a camera. No matter what happens now these little granules of colour will ensure that I live forever.

***

Louise Stone lives in Leicestershire. She is married to Paula. This is her first piece of writing. Louise runs creative mindfulness workshops and is a Life and Mindset Coach. Louise also works full time for the NHS:

https://www.facebook.com/louisestoneartandminds/

THIS IS AFRICA

Zoe Brooks

She was coming up again. This time she really needed to get away from the raft. She was almost out of air and energy. The torrent of water was keeping her under the raft. She couldn't swim in front and she couldn't seem to come up behind it either. Was this it? Two weeks into her African 'sort your life out' and 'find yourself' adventure, 'girl drowns in rafting accident', actually, no that would be woman and it might say 'midlife crisis adventure'. She tried to put her arms up and push the raft up, or at least away, but she couldn't touch the bottom of the fast-flowing river to get any kind of leverage. She was taking in a lot of water now and it was starting to hurt. She was left scrabbling, sinking and out of hope. Just as if someone had watched her give up, she felt a sharp pull on the back of her life jacket. Yes!!! She was being pulled away from the sodding raft and quite astoundingly thrown on top of it. Whilst coughing, retching and gulping huge breaths of air, she surveyed her saviour. One eye hazel and one eye blue, with dark hair, also luckily quite a large chap as he'd managed to pull her out from under the capsized raft onto the top of it in one swift movement. For many this would be the start of a romantic liaison or something; not here, though, she'd come here to get away from the opposite sex. She said a very sincere thank you very much and tried to compose herself.

After dinner, the majority of the group were in the campsite bar, sharing stories of their day out rafting, plenty of exaggerating, stories of bravery, cunning stunts and heroism. He was surrounded by the usual group of girls. She wondered if he'd even realised how long she'd been trying to get out from under the raft? Nothing was said about her rescue and she left it that way for now. She decided to sit with the group but at the edge so she could get onto the WIFI and check her emails but still appear to be joining in. She wasn't really in the mood for socialising but it was early in the tour and she needed to make an effort to get to know the group or it was going to be a lonely trip. She absentmindedly clicked on the Facebook app. There were a couple of messages from her mum checking she hadn't been eaten by a croc whilst rafting, and her mates asking if she was out on Friday – clearly they hadn't been paying much attention! She replied to Mum, neglecting to mention the near-death incident. Then he popped up… 'Hiya, you okay over there? What time is it?' She almost laughed at her own reaction. A couple of years ago she would have been delighted by Ian's eagerness and messaged straight back, but so much had changed. Maybe he was drunk or high… Either way, it certainly wasn't like him!

They had recently acknowledged the twelfth year of their on/off relationship, their fifth year of living together, but nothing ever progressing, no savings, no holidays, no weekends away as he might miss a gig. A couple of months before, everything had changed. She had started looking at Chris from work a bit differently, they'd been chatting more; they'd always been friends but it was something he'd said at 'after work drinks'. All of the people with places to go, other halves to meet, table reservations, tea to cook, had drunk up and gone. All that was left were the singles with no better plans. He'd apologised more or less straightaway, but he was right. They were standing in the smoking area of the pub across the road from work. It was cheap and cheerful, and the evening was warm. The kind of evening where everyone in London hits the pub and tries to get a seat outside. He'd asked where Ian was, he already knew the answer, where he always was, on a gig. He was a musician, a very talented one, but that came at a price. He was terrible at saying no to anyone but her. He could not miss a gig.

'Are you out for the duration then?'

'Erm, yeah, I guess I'll stay out a bit longer.'

'Any plans this weekend?'

'No, nothing big, it's wedding season, so Ian's packed out with gigs.'

Chris nodded in acknowledgement and talked about a festival he'd got tickets for in one of the parks. 'Why don't you come? Seems a shame to be sitting about on your own? You're more than welcome.'

'I'm not on my own,' she'd responded a little too quickly.

'You wouldn't be if you were mine.' He'd almost mumbled but she'd heard it and she felt like she'd been slapped. He looked at her, shrugged, threw his cigarette butt into the bin and walked off. 'Vodka and coke?' he asked without turning around.

'Yeah, okay, thanks!' she stood open mouthed.

The sound of glass smashing brought her back to the campsite bar in Uganda. One of the girls was getting a bit squiffy and wanted to arm-wrestle the boys (the good-looking ones – classic move). She looked up and laughed, quickly typed, 'I'm fine, thanks, all good,' and joined in the fun. No point sitting staring at your phone when you've a continent to explore.

The tour progressed. She was slowly starting to get to know the other group members but kept her cards close to her chest. The camping, meals and travelling on the truck had started to get into a routine. She had got better at organising her backpack, figuring out what to wear and keeping her day pack organised. She was also keeping a diary; she needed to savour every day and every experience that she was so fortunate to have. She was truly loving every minute. One particular Australian girl, Cat, also generally her tent/room buddy, liked asking questions; not just chit chat, pretty delving ones. 'So, what are you running away from?' Cat had said as she lit her cigarette and offered her one.

'Just work and responsibility,' she'd replied rather unconvincingly. They were sitting on the balcony of a rustic tree house looking over Lake Bunyonyi, surrounded by their own drying trousers, underwear and t-shirts, drinking warm rum and coke. She looked out at the sun shining on the lake. 'I guess I need to make some decisions when I get home about a few things, but nothing huge'. She'd tried to sound dismissive.

'Ah, I see, you've got a bit of a dilemma back home then?' This time she just smiled in response. 'You've got two on the go, haven't you?! Lucky girl! How'd ya manage that?!' How the hell did she guess that? Her face must have said exactly what she thought. 'Well,' said Cat smiling. 'I'd love to say it was my natural intuition, but I saw you making a list of pros and cons for each guy on the truck.' She couldn't deny that. She'd been using the long drive days to think about her 'situation' and how she'd even got into this mess.

Back to that hazy summer evening in Hammersmith, West London. They'd gone back to join the rest of the group like nothing had been said, but the seed had been planted. She found herself quietly wondering what life might be like with Chris. He liked to travel too, maybe they could set up a business together. She bet he'd be up for festivals, eating out, weekends away! Pets, kids even! Wow, wow, getting carried away there, but it posed the question: why wasn't Ian? They never did anything, their lives revolved around his gigs. Had they just been together all this time because they'd just gotten used to it? They had nothing in common and both knew no different and just accepted that was how life would be.

A tray of multiple small glasses filled with clear liquid had been placed in front of her and her remaining colleagues. 'SHOTS anyone?!' The new sales manager was keen to win some sort of alpha male title within the office. It was tequila, not her favourite, but better than sambuca. The group decided to move on to a new bar with some music and cocktails, after a quick snack at McDonald's. The bar was loud so it didn't permit much in the way of conversation but spirits were high and the group was having a great time. *I'm going to go to the festival with him tomorrow*, she thought. She texted him her response as he couldn't hear what she was saying. The reply came back instantly: a wink. Later, they stumbled towards the bus stop, he reached for her hand and she didn't pull it away. He stood up whilst she had the last seat on the N207. He held her hand again to the corner of her road and before it got awkward and anyone spoke, he pulled her to him and kissed her. Again, she didn't pull away. It could have been the cocktails, but her legs went weak, the world around them seemed to stop spinning. Is this the kind of kiss they try to recreate in films? In those books that her nana read?

She woke with a banging head to the sound of multiple things falling out of the cupboard in the living room of her flat. She lay there for a second, recalling the previous night. There was a pint of water and some painkillers by her side. Ian. Oh God, she was a dreadful person. She was sitting up in bed with the water as Ian more or less fell through the door with a suitcase (eh?). 'Hiya! Big night, was it? Ha ha! You were dead to the world when I got in, figured you'd need those.'

She mumbled something along the lines of the tequila shots. 'I'll get you a brew in a minute, is this the biggest bag we've got?'

'Erm, yes probably that one.' She sat, still dazed.

He laughed at her puzzled expression. 'I've been so excited to tell you. I've been offered a tour with Todd Edge, the guy who won that TV talent show. It's all over Europe, but it begins tomorrow night in London, so I'm thinking I'll do this wedding gig in Shrewsbury tonight then stay at Will's, as he's driving, then we fly out of Heathrow in the morning.' He was talking very fast, almost thinking out loud, babbling even. It really was great to see him so happy.

'That's great,' she managed with a big smile.

'Sorry it's such short notice, this is such a huge deal for me, I hope you're okay with this?'

'Oh yes, of course, honestly I'm just really hungover. I'm delighted for you, well done!'

'How many sets of clean pants have I got, do you reckon? Have you seen my passport? I'll get you that brew, shall I?' He more or less skipped out of the room, he was delighted, bless him. How could she tell him, would he even care? Of course he would! How could she do that to him? Maybe it was just a kiss and Chris was now sitting at home shuddering at the thought of it.

Actually, what about her? Her mood changed slightly. He was going to be away for her birthday; he wouldn't make Isla's wedding either. Would she spend the rest of her life being dumped last minute for months at a time? Was he going to pay the rent? Was it a paid gig? Now she was being selfish, or was he? Was she okay with this because she felt guilty. She decided to keep quiet and let him enjoy the moment. They could sort rent and the rest of it online or over the phone.

By lunchtime, after a pretty unceremonious goodbye, he'd gone. The flat was trashed where he'd been searching for things, adding them to his case then taking them out. She looked at her phone for the first time that day. There was a message from Chris. 'Sorry if I overstepped the mark last night. I genuinely do think the world of you. I still have a spare ticket if you're keen. No pressure and no more funny stuff, though.' She was dressed and feeling surprisingly okay. She went to meet Chris and his mates at Marble Arch tube station. In the month that followed, things progressed and, in all honesty, she just stopped thinking. Thinking was hard and it hurt. She was having the best time with Chris, bike riding, in the pub, eating out, just wandering around exploring London on the weekends, just like any other couple in love. Yes, she was in love.

Ian's space on the tour had been extended, his texts had become far less frequent, and in fairness so had her own. She'd been following the pictures of the tour on Facebook and Instagram at the beginning, but she'd lost interest. It wasn't her world, or her dream. He'd paid the rent two weeks late but she'd managed. She was going to tell him. She was going to call him and tell him tonight after work. An email popped up requesting a meeting at work. It was from the director. In between profanities it seemed that one of the truck drivers in Africa had quit and the other had been in a bar fight. He wanted two new drivers and two back-up drivers on standby. In the meeting that followed it was deemed that the best course of action was for someone to go out there, interview them at one or two of the main campsites, ensure their papers were in order and go through some training with the successful candidates. She offered to do it on the spot on the condition that she combined it with joining one of the tours. Maybe this was the opportunity she needed to make some big decisions for herself. By close of business, the flights were booked, candidates emailed, and she was joining an overland tour in Uganda, travelling down to South Africa. She'd used up some accrued annual leave, a fair bit of goodwill and in total she would be away for two months.

That night, on the phone to Ian, she decided not to mention there being another person involved. Instead she just tried to be honest about how their relationship had changed and how she had felt before Chris had turned up. Ian sounded bright and cheery but distant; he was having the time of his life, who could blame him! The last thing he needed was a moaning girlfriend talking about her feelings. She told him about the trip and when she'd be back. As things currently stood, he'd probably get back at about the same time. They agreed it wasn't necessarily working at present and that they'd discuss it in person when they both got back. A huge weight had been lifted; she had not been entirely truthful, but it was a step in the right direction. Chris' reaction was slightly less indifferent, but he acknowledged her trip to be a great opportunity, then hugged her so tight she thought she might stop breathing!

She'd never been a morning person until she came to Africa. Here, it was the coolest part of the day, when the wildlife was most active. She loved getting up early with her torch, getting the stove lit and the first kettle of water boiling, then she just sat with her coffee and watched the campsite and her surroundings wake up. Today the group were on an early game drive in the Maasai Mara. The plan was to find the lions with their kill. The local guides had been tracking a pride of lionesses since yesterday evening and, if their excited discussions via the radio were anything to go by, this would be a big deal. Cameras poised and fully charged, the group took picture after picture of the bloody carcass of a zebra being torn and devoured. Close by, a bush was wobbling. The guide shushed everyone; they almost held their breath until out popped a little fluffy head. Then a huge paw and another head, followed by a blurred fuzzy ball as the two cubs lost their balance and rolled out of the shelter of the bush.

On the way back to the campsite, her mobile rang.

It was Ian; she nearly dropped it. She'd had no contact from him for a while. She answered sounding surprised but friendly.

'Hiya!'

'Hi.' He sounded subdued, maybe drunk? She had no idea. 'We've had an email from the letting agent, they're ending our tenancy. We've got three months to move out.'

'Okay, what date?'

'Erm, I'm not sure, I'll just forward it. Anyway, I guess I'll just move back in with my mum after this. I've got to go now, afterparty and all that.' He hung up, not waiting for her to respond. She sat for a minute where she had stood, suddenly overcome with regret and a deep sadness. She was back in the grounds of the campsite, so no wild animals. Was this it? Twelve years of hanging around and waiting. What had she waited for? A proposal? A mortgage? A weekend away? As if to rescue her from her own feelings of resentment, Cat appeared. 'Jeez, these bottles are cold, hurry up, take one off me!' She laughed at her tent mate. It was barely lunchtime. 'I'm not going to ask what you're doing lurking in the bushes but I'm guessing you had some sort of breakthrough with your dilemma. Have you got any tampons?'

They had by now played every card game known to man. This was quite possibly the longest, hottest 'drive day' ever. Cat had decided to open the cooler. 'Is it okay to have a 'sundowner' when you haven't been on a safari?'

'Yes!' came the chorus from the back of the truck. Beers were distributed, the cards put away and the driver put some music on. The tour leader got on the microphone to announce their arrival into Livingstone, Zambia. 'We're going to have to stop off near the airport and get fuel then we'll head straight to camp.' They pulled in at the airport, no petrol station seemingly close by. 'One sec,' shouts the tour leader as he jumps out of the truck. 'Got to get something!' The group were singing by the time the tour leader emerged, his arm around someone familiar, carrying their backpack. She knew him! She knew him and she actually loved him, and he had flown to Zambia, for her, to be with her! She jumped out of the truck and into his arms. They fit together perfectly and today they still do.

★★★

Zoe Brooks is originally from Chesterfield, currently living in Market Harborough after seven years in London working for an adventure travel tour operator. She is a mum of one and a rabbit. She now works as a Virtual Assistant, specialising in social media, online content creation, travel planning and business development. This story does not condone cheating or dishonesty but if you take anything away from this let it be that life is too short not to follow your heart and be happy:

https://linktr.ee/ZoeBrooksVirtualAssistant

MAGGIE'S ADVENTURE

Kirsty France

"If I hadn't been up with the baby, I would have missed her." Louise turned away from the detective sergeant as the kettle boiled. "Are you sure I can't get you a hot drink?"

"I'm fine, thanks."

Louise made herself a strong black coffee and picked up the biscuits before sitting down at the kitchen table. "Sorry about that. We had a bad night last night and I'm basically surviving on caffeine and chocolate biscuits."

DS Angela Hobson smiled sympathetically, shaking her head at the offer of biscuits. Louise found herself wondering if the sergeant was a mum too. She looked smart in her suit but her short haircut and bare minimum make up spoke of someone who didn't have much time to get ready in the morning. Even so, Louise felt suddenly scruffy in comparison. She couldn't remember the last time her hair had seen a brush.

"Your husband isn't here at the moment, is he? Might he have seen anything?"

Louise snorted. "Not a chance! He's been wearing

earplugs for the last few nights. God forbid he misses a minute of sleep." She realised she sounded sharper than she had intended. "Sorry. Lack of sleep makes me catty."

Hobson smiled. "That's okay. Can you take me through what you saw?"

Louise took a deep breath before she spoke. She was about to give a complete stranger all the details of her closest friend's life and it suddenly seemed a lot more difficult than she'd thought. She told DS Hobson about how she'd been up with her teething baby and had headed to the kitchen for more Calpol. She watched her smile as she described the way that living at the bottom of a cul-de-sac had turned her into a nosy neighbour.

"I can see the whole of the close from here, all the comings and goings. Well, you can see for yourself." She gestured towards the kitchen window and watched as DS Hobson took in the view. "The perils of being a bored housewife."

"You're sure it was Maggie Henderson?"

"Absolutely positive. I wasn't at first because she was carrying one of those big camping rucksacks. They never went camping. But then the security light at number fourteen lit up as she passed. She looked round and I saw her quite clearly. We've been friends since Neil and I moved in. The other neighbours are friendly enough, but they're either out at work all day or a lot older than us. We hit it off straight away." Maggie was the kind of friend that Louise had always wanted but never had. Someone you could watch 'Thelma and Louise' with, giggling your heads off through mouthfuls of pizza and generic white wine. "I thought it might be awkward when I had Luke, but it was fine." Louise registered the sergeant's understanding nod. Of course. Stuart was bound to have told them that they had been trying for a baby. Louise could almost hear him making the report, telling the police about the strain that it had put on both of them. Of course, Neil had been the fount of all wisdom on that one. Louise had cringed as she watched Neil take Stuart to one side for a 'man to man' chat the last time they came over for a barbecue. Maggie had just rolled her eyes.

"Did you see which way she went?"

Louise shook her head. "She just walked up the close. She was on the right-hand pavement so she might have turned that way, but I couldn't see."

"And that was what time?"

"Just after 3am."

"My brother calls it the witching hour."

Louise smiled. "You hear parents talk about it, then you become one and find out exactly what they mean. I don't know whether babies feel pain or loneliness more intensely in the middle of the night, or whether it's because we're less able to deal with it."

"Maybe both." Hobson smiled. "Actually, maybe I will have a biscuit, if that's okay?"

Louise proffered the biscuit tin again and took one herself. She had wondered how to begin telling DS Hobson the rest of her story, but somehow the shared conviviality of chocolate biscuits made it easier. Still, there was a lump in her throat that she had to swallow before she could speak. She found herself lowering her voice, as though there was someone else listening in. She asked whether they had any information about why Maggie had walked out of her house in the middle of the night. The sergeant shook her head, as Louise had known she would.

"It's okay. I know you couldn't tell me even if you did, but that's all right. I suspect I already know." Hobson's look of surprise told Louise that Maggie hadn't left a note, after all. *You do love to keep people guessing, don't you lovely one?* "The thing is, I'm not sure she wants to be found."

Louise had been amazed at how freely the words flowed once she began to speak. She told DS Hobson about the times she'd gone round to find Maggie raging because Stuart had been on at her to go for ever more weird and wonderful fertility tests because the GP wouldn't help; they hadn't been trying for long enough. Or in tears because he blamed her. Stuart had even been round to ask Louise if Maggie was okay, because he was worried about her. That last barbecue, when Neil was dispensing yet more wisdom on how to achieve successful impregnation, had been the last straw.

Maggie had poured herself a massive glass of wine, ignoring Stuart's furious glare. She'd wrapped her arm around Louise's shoulders and kissed her on the cheek. 'Balls to the lot of them. Let's have a proper drink.' Louise had laughed in disbelief – this was the Maggie she knew and loved. They drank a toast and shared the last of the Sauvignon Blanc between them. By the time Maggie had leaned in and asked her if she could keep a secret, Louise's head was already swimming.

"So, she told you she was going to leave?"

"She said she was going to start again. I assumed that's what she meant." She watched as Hobson's expression changed. "Does that change things?"

"If she's gone of her own free will..."

"She has, I know she has. Wait, she's allowed to do that, isn't she?"

"As long as she's..." DS Hobson's voice trailed off. Her face showed that she'd been about to reveal too much.

Louise could almost feel the clunk as the penny dropped. Of course. Stuart had asked Louise about Maggie's mental state. If he was worried enough to ask her, why wouldn't he mention it to the police when she wandered off in the middle of the night? Louise had watched enough crime dramas to know that they don't go searching for adults who've been missing for less than twenty-four hours unless they were vulnerable. "He told you she was mad, didn't he? Stuart?"

"You know I can't tell you that," Hobson replied. "Let's just say there was evidence to suggest that she might have caused herself harm."

Louise shook her head wearily. "Look, I can't tell you if she walked out of the village and threw herself into the nearest lake. But she told me she wanted a fresh start then she packed a bag. It seems like an awful lot of effort if you're going to end it all."

"Thanks for your time. And the biscuits." Hobson spoke as Louise opened the front door. "If there's anything else..."

"I've got your card."

Louise heard Luke let out a hungry cry as she closed the door and checked her watch. Good. Plenty of time before Neil came home. She climbed the stairs, passing the rucksacks on the landing on the way to his room. The cry was getting louder.

"It's okay, lovely boy, Mummy's here." She heard the footsteps behind her as she lifted him from the cot. "We're almost ready to go. He just needs a nappy change and a snack."

She turned to see Maggie smiling at her, ready for their new adventure.

***

Kirsty France is a copywriter from Leicestershire. She provides copywriting services including blog writing to small businesses all over the world. In her spare time, she attempts to turn her two young sons into civilised human beings and watches quizzes with her husband. This is her first published work of fiction but she's currently working on her first crime novel: www.kirstyfrancewrites.co.uk

NO LOVE LOST

Paris Booton

I was standing at the bar of a quiet pub. The walls were lined with alcohol bottles, either clear or dark, creating a gloomy atmosphere across the bar. The bar was wet with spilled drinks whilst the barman held a conversation with a balding man.

There was a tap on my shoulder.

I turned around and I was greeted with a wry smile, a familiar face, a blast from the past.

"In all the gin joints, in all the towns in all the world… yada yada yada. How are you doing?" Before I knew it, I was pulled into a hug. A faint odour of vodka hung from him, along with a strong smell of smoke.

"Hey. Fancy seeing you here, Jared. I'm good, how are you?" I replied, whilst examining his face. His eyes looked less vibrant than I remembered. His face, once smoothed, looked more leathery. He was only twenty-five but I was comparing to the fresh-faced eighteen-year-old I knew. It didn't look like the years had been kind.

"Yeah, I'm good." There was an awkward silence,

there were no right words to say to him. It'd been seven years since I saw him in the back of a Toyota Corolla with a burn on the back seat behind the passenger side. I looked past him to the fruit machine; watching the array of lights. I looked down at my feet, letting my red curls fall from my shoulder to then fold them behind my ears.

His hands came out of his pockets and quickly went back in again. I thought he seemed nervous.

"This is weird, right? It's been seven years. You've not changed though. You're still as beautiful as ever, Alana." I sighed and shifted my weight onto my other hip. My name rolled off his tongue like it had never left, it was disconcerting but oddly comforting.

"Yeah, I guess. It's a bit weird. Blast from the past though, right?"

"Yeah," he said, sadly. Though I'm not sure why he was sad. Things didn't end badly between us, it just ended. At least from his perspective. I was heartbroken; he blocked me and moved on fast from what I had heard.

"Hey, this may sound weird but—" He was cut off by a slender man coming up to the bar, his red shirtsleeves rolled up, his black hair tussled, his face had sagging under the eyes and just an overall listlessness. He was so tired.

"Hey, babe." The red-sleeved man walked up behind me, my body language angled towards him at the sound of his voice. Jared looked away and stroked his hand through his hair. "Who's this?"

"Oh, he's..." I began.

"Leaving. See you later, Alana," Jared said as he cut me off. He turned and left through the door to the car park behind him. I watched as he left. Joss leant over the bar again to grab the drink he had ordered.

Joss never brought up Jared again.

The next morning, Joss was still in bed when I arose and fumbled to the bathroom, dragging a skirt and shirt that felt more like a heavy weight from a science class than pieces of fabric. I looked in the mirror and looked at the curves around my hips and the tattoo around my belly button; a reminder of the life before. I dressed and ran a brush through my hair.

"I've got to go, Al. I'm going to be late. You okay?" shouted Joss; he must have got out of bed quietly. Maybe I was too lost in my thoughts to register the sounds.

"Yeah, I'll see you later. I love you."

"Love you too," shouted Joss as he left the flat.

I placed my heels on the floor and slipped my feet into them. As I stood, I wobbled whilst I found my gravity. I smoothed down my skirt. I kept replaying the scene from last night. I thought further back to when we were eighteen; the way we laughed together; when we would meet at 2pm and spend the rest of the night together. I felt a pain in my chest, a heaviness. I let out a loud sigh to release the pressure and walked out of the door.

I thought walking through the door would thrust me into the real world but it didn't, my mind was still stuck in the past. I stepped on the bus and I made the whole journey on muscle memory alone. I stepped off the bus and looked for my phone in my bag. As I looked up, my eyes met the dark eyes of a familiar face.

"Wha... Jared?"

"Hey, Al," articulated Jared.

"What are you doing here?" I asked him incredulously.

"Last night, seeing you, just brought back a lot of old memories. Fancy going somewhere?" I looked down at the skirt, shirt, heels and handbag – all massive signs that I had somewhere else to be.

"Look, I don't know what kind of mid-twenties crisis you are having but I have work," I mocked as I pushed past him. Jared spun round and walked alongside me.

"You're not going to outrun me in heels." He laughed. I chuckled at him.

"Anything you can do, I can do in heels. If I wanted to run in heels, I could." He laughed, I didn't find it cute.

"Yeah, well... C'mon. Skip work." Jared playfully tapped my arm. "Just one day. It'll be fun!" I hadn't had much fun in the last few years. In fact, the last time I could pinpoint a 'fun' period in my life was back with Jared. I half smiled at him.

"Okay. As friends."

"As friends." We walked down the road to his car. It was a Ford Focus.

"What happened to the Corolla?" I laughed as I went round to the passenger front seat. He coyly laughed.

"Just felt it was time to get rid of it," answered Jared.

"That's a shame."

He drove fast down the dual carriageway.

"Where are we going?" I asked, kicking myself for not asking sooner.

"Back to where we began."

I started replaying a memory in my head:

Meeting up with my friend in the town over from ours, she had brought someone she knew. He was beautiful, he was tall and he had that kind of emotional range that makes older me ashamed I ever entertained him.

Katie, Jared and I wandered around town. We talked about the places we'd go when we were eighteen. We could go to all those places now; the beach, Blackpool, the movies. But imagine how cool it would be as adults. Fully fledged adults. That we'd waited our whole lives to be. I looked at Jared. With his short brown hair, seafoam-coloured eyes and a warm undertone to his skin. He had his hood up and his hands stuck in his pockets.

"I'm going to have to go," mused Katie as she put her bag over a shoulder. She curved up her lips in a directed smile towards me. She was hoping now would be the point Jared and I would finally get together.

"Okay, get home safely," I shouted as Katie walked down the street. She turned around and waved.

"Do you need to leave too?" asked Jared.

"No."

"I want to go to the supermarket," murmured Jared. "Want to come?" I watched as Jared pulled out a cigarette. He lit it and offered one to me. I shook my head.

Jared pulled the car into the car park of the

supermarket. We caught eyes as he undid his seatbelt. I hastily undid mine. He stepped out of the car, I fought to get out smoothly in heels. Jared was waiting at the front of the car and pulled up the hood on his hoodie. He continued to walk to the store as I tried to keep pace.

"Do you remember the last time we were here?" Asked Jared. I chuckled at the memory.

"Yeah. When they made us show both IDs because you wanted cider. Good thing I had it." Jared laughed harder.

"Lucky that. You always were a bit of an airhead though." An uncomfortable pressure rose in my chest. The criticism that came from Jared's mouth felt all too familiar.

"I wouldn't say that," I retorted. He laughed again. Jared walked down the centre of the supermarket until he got to the alcohol aisle. I caught a sight of myself in the security camera. My shirt was creased from where I'd been slouching in the car. My posture, usually stiff and straight, was slouched as I fought to keep up with Jared. He picked up a bottle of cider and headed for the tills.

"Do you think they'll ask for our IDs again?" he jested.

"Is it an insult or a compliment if they do?" I asked.

Jared laughed again, I smiled and looked down to the floor. He paid for the bottle and we headed back to the car.

Jared tossed the bottle on the back seat and sat down

in the front seat. He took out another cigarette and placed it in the cup holder.

"Still smoking?" I asked.

"Until it kills me." He replied. I turned to look out of the passenger window, waiting for that same uncomfortable feeling to pass.

"Mind if I turn on the radio?" I asked.

"Have at it." I fiddled with the buttons. Love Song by Sara Bareilles came on the radio. I dwelled on old memories as I gazed at the trees whizzing past.

Sitting on the bus, Sara Bareilles was blasting through my headphones. I was filled with the budding excitement that I was experiencing for the first time. Was I in love? What was it? Whatever it is, it was fun. Jared had just got off shift and we were meeting at his house. Travelling back and forth between my house and his, romantic kisses and sweet nothings were all new to me. It's a teenage romance and I was finally glad to be experiencing it.

Jared reached over and was feeling the buttons of the radio; it brought me back to the present.

"What are you doing?" I scrunched up my face as I asked.

"We're not going to listen to this, are we?" Jared smirked.

"I would think so, Jared. I like this song." Jared shrugged his shoulders.

"Whatever, you can listen to your bad music and then we'll pick something good." I turned towards the window and watched as the trees whizzed past. Jared tapped my leg. "You're not mad at me, are you?" I smiled to hide my discomfort.

Jared slowed down as we reached the town centre. Sara Bareilles sang about walking the seven seas as he pulled up. Facing us was a cluster of benches.

"Remember that?" asked Jared. I stared hard at the benches as I recalled the memory.

"Oh... Is that where we met up when Katie and I came up to see you?"

"You remember." He smirked. "I'm surprised that you would, it was a while ago." I shifted in my seat.

"You know, I've missed you." They were words I was longing to hear. After the break up, Jared ghosted me. He never explained why we broke up. I always thought I'd want to hear those words. I'd think back to Jared and wonder what could have been. What I ever meant to him. I always wanted closure.

"Jared, I've got a boyfriend. Joss, at the bar, last night." Jared took hold of my hand.

"I've missed you, Alana. I made a mistake. Sometimes it takes a while to realise your mistake. We had a good thing going... Don't you want to find out what could have been?"

My heart swelled. That is all I wanted to hear all those years ago.

"I won't lie, I've always wondered and we did have fun."

"We did have fun," he reiterated.

"Jared—" He cut me off, sensing my hesitancy.

"Look, don't say anything yet. Let me take you to one more place."

Jared pulled the car up in the cul-de-sac, outside a house with a dark green door.

"Isn't this your parents' house?" I wondered aloud.

"Yeah, my mum and dad always liked you," replied Jared. I smiled. I always liked his family. They were sweet and funny and made me feel included.

"I liked them too." Jared got out of the car and headed towards the house. He didn't even turn to check I was following.

"Guess I'm struggling out of the car alone again," I muttered to the empty space. I hobbled out of the car again and caught up with Jared before he managed to open the door. The door opened and released the familiar smell of cigarette smoke. As we entered through the front door, I remembered how the house used to look. An eighties celebrity donned the walls in the hall and up the stairs. The floor leading to the kitchen was linoleum, trying to display dark wooden planks. Jared led me through to the sitting room; the floor was wooden planks, worn but recently polished.

Sitting on a green armchair was Jared's dad. His hair had greyed more since the last time I saw him, his skin sagged from his face and his glasses sat on the bridge of his nose. His mum was still slim, but was frailer since the last time I saw her. His mum greeted me with a hug like she did the first time she met me.

"Oh, you're still so beautiful!" she gushed. I smiled as she held me at arm's length.

"She is a looker," agreed Jared's dad, admiring from his chair.

"We've missed you," she whispered.

"I missed you too."

"Mum!" groaned Jared from the hallway. "Let's go upstairs, Al."

We climbed up the stairs and I admired the celebrity's pictures.

"Things don't change, huh?" mused Jared. I stayed silent. We reached his room and he opened the door. I followed behind, and a strong smell of aftershave still lingered in his room. His room was still full of football team merchandise.

"I thought you didn't massively like football?"

"I don't. But if it's not broke, don't fix it." He sat on the bed and patted next to him. I sat down on the edge of the bed, I didn't even remove my heels. *Why wouldn't I remove my heels? I remove them in the office which is way less formal than this.* Jared scooted next to me.

"Your parents seem well, I'm so glad." I exclaimed. He got out a cigarette again. He stroked his hand up my arm.

"Yeah… It's weird being back here again, isn't it?"

I thought back to the first time I was here:

The TV rolled credits as Jared and I shared our first kiss. I stroked back my hair. Jared stopped and put something else on the TV. I felt happy and excited. My heart beat fast. Jared went to kiss me again.

"Give me a second to catch my breath." I laughed. Jared sighed loudly.

His reaction made me uncomfortable; this was supposed to be making me happy. 'Don't get hung up on silly stuff,' I told myself.

"It's definitely something," I replied as I snapped back to the present.

"But it feels right, doesn't it?" He edged closer towards me. I uncomfortably looked to the door. He hooked my chin with his finger to get eye contact. "I really have missed you." He leaned closer to me and before I could react, he kissed me. I flung myself backwards.

"What the hell? I have a boyfriend."

"So what? You wouldn't have come if that mattered."

"It does matter. I came because I wanted closure over what happened. But why do I need it? You were immature then, you're immature now. You care very little about my wellbeing. Joss would help me when I'm in heels and would slow his pace so I wasn't walking alone. You never cared about that. I'm the idiot who was following around some teenage dream." The closure I needed wasn't why he broke up with me, it was realising that I should have chosen me; chosen the healthy choice. There was no choice between Jared and Joss. If the choice was Jared and nothing, it should be nothing. Joss was who I loved. I may not live that fun, carefree life anymore, but Joss made the hard things fun.

The love was in the little gestures, not in the one who caused the most heartbreak.

"Al…"

"I'm going now, Jared."

I walked down the stairs and bumped into his mum.

"I heard the commotion upstairs. You coming down like this reminds me of last time; you crying that day," Jared's mum remarked.

"Yeah, I remember that but I think I'm over that now."

"You should have been over it a long time ago. You deserve better. I hope to see you again, darling." I walked out of the door and down the street to the bus stop. The only thing I wanted was to get to there. To the bus stop I used to walk to alone at 11pm, to get the last bus home. The hour-long bus back to where I needed to be. I was glad to be doing it for the last time.

When I was finally home, I opened the front door to the home Joss and I shared. The lights were off. I turned them on and followed a trail of sunflowers in vases to the kitchen. I could smell something cooking.

"Joss?" I called into the house.

Joss came out, he was wearing a jumper and jeans.

"Al, I was going to wait. Until later, until I could make it perfect, but life isn't perfect. I just want to be with you."

He pulled out a ring from his back pocket.

"Will you marry me?"

★★★

Paris Booton runs her own business in Leicester. She parents two little ones and they've been surviving and sometimes thriving. It's been a dream of hers to get a piece of fiction published since she wrote a twelve-page story for design class in year seven. Check out more at:

sunflowerfamilies.co.uk

VANILLA

Kate Jordin

The way she always ate the same crisps in the same way, nibbled ridge by ridge, making them last about twenty minutes. The way she then folded the packet into a neat triangle with a small, satisfied smile. The way she twisted her hair to lie over her shoulder when she wore it down. The way she touched a person's arm when she laughed at something they said.

All these little things that he had found so endearing, so alluring when he first met her, now made him clench his jaw. Made him want to throw things at her.

He longed for a dalliance, something risqué. They'd watched a film a while back, and this couple had just fallen into this crazy, passionate affair. It had all looked so easy. All it had taken was just one simple glance. He had given it a lot of thought, and wondered if it was maybe just a case of maximising opportunities.

He reasoned that he was not bad looking, despite the unfortunate hair. It had been trained over many, many years into the same boring style, and there was no way now it was ever going to break out into anything else. His eyes had once been described as 'sensuous brown' and he had pretty good biceps. He had a cute chin dimple. He wasn't hideous.

So he started to take the tube instead of walking to work. In the frantic commuter rush, he could be just one of the many fleeting bodies that would brush and push so close to one another, sometimes able to graze a breast, a buttock with the back of his hand, without reproach. He would often pick out a woman and stare at the back of her head, imagining her turning to see him looking, raising an eyebrow, a flirty smile playing on her lips… inviting him to follow her to a secluded corner somewhere.

His attempts at maximising opportunities at work had mostly only served to alienate rather than entice his female colleagues. Though he did not know it, they had gifted him the nickname of 'Scary, Starey Steve' due to his insistence on maintaining full eye contact during a conversation. All he had ever managed was *almost* meeting up for a quick lunchtime fumble with Lorraine from purchasing in the disabled toilet. The culmination of two months of slightly awkward flirty emails. That had been disappointing in every way.

It had, however, opened his eyes to possibilities, and after a day of talking himself into it, he set up an email address under the pseudonym of Phil Darkley and posted an advert on a casual hook-up site. The rush of excitement when he saw it there in black and white had made him feel liberated at first, but when Phil Darkley's inbox started to fill up with replies, he was so terrified that he deleted them all without reading them.

He gradually started spending more time at the gym, envisaging a heated encounter in the steam room, or an accidentally placed hand in the jacuzzi. His friend Rob introduced him to spin classes, and now Steve tried to go at least three times a week. He liked to get in early and claim the bike at the back that offered the best view of all the toned glutes thrusting in front of him, for a blissful forty-five minutes. It was a painful workout if the plan backfired, however, when it was the overweight middle-aged clumpies who parked their backsides in front of him instead.

He sometimes took the long way home after spin class so he could pass the local park's semi-secluded car park. He didn't really understand what dogging was exactly, only that it often happened at night in semi-secluded car parks. He remembered seeing a story in the paper once, local uproar, that kind of thing. He once felt brave enough to drive in and park up, hands shaking on the steering wheel the whole time. But the only other car there had been full of teenagers getting stoned.

Occasionally he would feel disgusted with himself, and would worry that he was a pervert. He was sure he wasn't, though; wasn't the fact he worried about it proof enough that he wasn't? Plus he had never once watched pornography, and didn't all perverts spend hours watching pornography?

Lacking confidence, a bit quirky, he had been a late

starter with girls. By the age of twenty-one, there had only ever been one other girlfriend when he met Janey. He had been utterly blown away by her confidence, her sexual prowess, her absolute self-possession. He had become lost in her, at one with her every thought and action. She seduced him, pursued him even… but now he spent nearly every evening in the same tug of war with her; him trying to get laid, her too busy getting the dinner ready, putting the kids to bed, getting lunches ready for the morning and then too busy being tired from being too busy. When it did happen, it was perfunctory. Tame, silent, polite.

Most nights he would lie awake and plot his seduction of the stunning dark-haired girl he had once seen getting off the tube at Temple. Steve would catch her eye whilst always saying the same thing; a silly schoolboy nonsense about her body being the temple that he would pray at every day. Of course, the tube train of his fantasy was always empty and she would always smile at him, and he would move towards her, reach out to her and then… his alarm would go off. And she would slink away from his grasp once more.

The frustration of his thwarted passion was easier to bear in the warmer months. He loved that first warm day of spring, but not, as he pretended to Janey, because of the swifts and swallows. Somehow she had never noticed that whilst his binoculars were always on the bedroom windowsill, the copy of *British Birds to Spot in Your Garden* she had given him for his birthday last year still stood, spine unbent and pages stiff, in the bookcase in the lounge.

No, spring meant there would soon be the promise of skirts skimming tanned thighs, bikini tops, drops of sweat on collarbones. Unfortunately, it also meant hot pants on fat girls who should know better, but to Steve that was a price worth paying.

In summer, he would spend his lunch-break skirting the patch of green outside the offices where he could stare unseen from behind his dark glasses as the grass filled up with delicious bodies trying to get a forty-five minute tan.

He would wait. Just hoping for that look, that one simple glance.

When he came home he would kiss Janey and the kids, he would watch her with them and how they would all show off a little to get his attention. He sometimes saw that flash in her eyes when she looked up at him, but he knew now that it was no longer for him.

And as they sat down to watch TV and she opened her bag of crisps, he would yearn for something, anything, just any small way to make his life a little bit more flavoursome, a little less vanilla.

★★★

Kate lives in Leicestershire and has two noisy and opinionated small boys. At 41 she is rediscovering her love for writing after some years concentrating on her other passion of cake and sugar art. She previously had poems published in similar anthologies, though this was in The Life Before Children:

https://www.thebakewelltart.com/

CALL IT OFF

Laura Lawrence

'Please will you call everyone and explain?'

'How can I explain something I don't understand myself? Rosie what has happened in the time it took me to go and collect your flowers?!'

Rosie drops her eye contact with me and plonks down onto the leather sofa beside us. She pulls her feet up onto the cushion and hugs her legs the way we used to when we pretended to be mushrooms in the swimming pool. I know I should remind her of our parents' rule of no feet on the sofa but she's acting so weirdly already.

'Daisy, what the heck has happened?'

Daisy looks from me to Rosie and back again but says nothing. Instead, she slides down next to Rosie and places an arm comfortingly around her shoulders. She looks up to me and her face says it all. She knows what's happening but she doesn't want to tell me in front of Rosie. I've always been able to read Daisy like a book but Rosie is the wild child. I have no idea what goes through her mind half the time and I hate that she keeps me on my toes so often.

'Maybe you could run Rosie a bath, Pops? A glass of wine and some chocolates on the side? Maybe a nice relaxing book?'

I scowl at my younger sister. Why is she telling me what to do and why am I to run a romantic bath for my youngest sister who has just asked me to call 'everyone' to cancel her wedding. Daisy responds to my scowl with a wide-eyed look that conveys 'do it and don't question it'. I roll my eyes but decide to follow the plan. Daisy is the nurturer, so she probably knows how best to deal with this situation.

'Fine, would you like some music as well, Rosie?'

Rosie keeps her head buried in her lap but her blonde mop of hair moves in a nodding action.

Once I had run the bath and set the bathroom up, it took everything in me to not jump in myself; the relaxing jasmine and ylang ylang bubble bath filled my lungs and the warmth of the water filled the small yellow and blue bathroom. I put on some Ed Sheeran then begrudgingly called my little sister up. Daisy has practically carried Rosie up the two flights of stairs into Rosie's en-suite bathroom in her loft bedroom. As soon as Rosie was in the bathroom, Daisy grabbed my hand and pulled me down into the bedroom that she and Rosie had shared until the loft extension gave her a room of her own.

'What is going on, Daisy?!'

'You will never believe this, I mean you'll probably tell me you saw it a mile off, but I'm still in shock and

I feel like I know Rosie better than you, I am the best sister after all!'

I roll my eyes good-naturedly at Daisy but I'm not denying she's the best, she keeps the three of us close and brings our sisterhood into friendships.

'Wow, just tell me already, Mum and Dad will be home soon!'

'Shut up and listen already! So, you know how Rosie and Travis had a whirlwind relationship and we were totally shocked that they were getting married so soon?'

'She's pregnant!? I am not ready to be an auntie yet, I was planning on getting pregnant after the wedding so I don't look fat in her wedding photos! If she's now gone and got pregnant just to get there first I will never forgive her!'

Daisy stares silently at me for what feels like forever. I can hear my own heart beating and the clock ticking but I'm not talking first.

'Right, well, that wasn't listening now, was it? So no, Rosie is not pregnant. Before you jump to conclusions, I'm not either, yeah, so you're safe for now. Although Pete did say he wanted to start trying soon…'

'Daisy!'

'I'm kidding, we've only been married a year, we aren't close to thinking about babies yet. Soooo Rosie.'

'Oh yeah, she will be out of the bath soon. Why did she just tell me AFTER I'd picked up her flowers that she's cancelling the wedding and I have the job of calling everyone? Has she even told Travis?'

Daisy leans in closer with a look of conspiracy. I can feel a weird tension come into the room and I feel like a teenager about to get some juicy gossip again.

'So, Rosie's bridesmaids are us and Fiona, right? Well… turns out Rosie likes Fiona more than she likes us.'

Daisy winks as she exaggerates the word 'likes'. This isn't juicy gossip, this is obvious.

'Well yeah, I love the two of you because you're my sisters and I'm stuck with you both forever, but I LIKE my best friend more than you two as well. Rosie and Fi have been best friends since uni.'

'No, no, Rosie LIKES Fi, as in likes her more than Travis.'

'Again, I like Annie more than Jai sometimes too, we have been friends longer than I've been married and we have more in common. We are basically married anyway other than the ring and sex!'

Daisy rolls her eyes and sighs at me like she thinks I'm an idiot.

'Okay, well the only thing Rosie and Fi are missing from their 'marriage' is the ring. Does that help you?'

'Whaaaat!?'

Daisy and I have been sitting on her old bed, edging closer without noticing it as we have been talking, so right now our foreheads are almost touching as we lean in to each other.

'Our baby sister likes females not males. She told me that Travis and her are great friends. He's been pressured by his parents to find a wife and start a family. She knew that Dad is too old fashioned to ever accept her as a lesbian, so she agreed to marry Travis to keep both sets of parents happy. This way they could have babies, which they both want, and parents that won't be disappointed. Apparently he knew she was with Fiona and was fine with her being a part of their life. This whole thing was just a show.'

'Shut up!! Did you know?!'

Daisy shakes her head and I can tell she's telling the truth.

'Fiona called her whilst you were out and said she doesn't want to be her maid of honour now, as she is just finding this whole situation too hard to deal with and she can't bear the thought of watching the woman she loves marry someone else, even if it's fake. She doesn't want to be part of the lie anymore, so she wants to split up; basically she gave Rosie an ultimatum and of course Rosie chose her.'

I stand up and start pacing the room. I can feel the blood pumping through my ears and the hairs are standing up on the back of my neck. Now I'm closer to the bedroom door I can hear the radio on downstairs and the rumble of the kettle heating up. This means that any minute now our mum will be on her way up with a tray full of tea and biscuits. Or she will at least call us down to join her.

'Mum's home, we don't have to tell her anything, right? Rosie will deal with this.'

Daisy jumps off the bed and comes to join me next to the door. We both listen hard. Rosie's music is still on upstairs, so she must still be in the bath.

'Right, one of us needs to go distract Mum and one needs to go drag Rosie down. Which do you want?'

'Mum?' Daisy shrugs nonchalantly but we both know she's got the easy task.

'Fine, come on, but say nothing to Mum and if Dad's home too then text me a warning.'

'Sure… good luck!'

I hate being the eldest sometimes. I feel like I've regressed back to my teenage years as I stomp up the stairs ready to tell my youngest sister to get out of the bath and come talk to Mum with me about the latest drama.

'Rosie, are you decent?'

There's no reply from my sister and I even knocked on her bedroom door, something none of us would have ever done growing up. I knock again but still there's no answer so instead I barge in, she's clearly still sulking in the bath.

Yep, as suspected, she's still in the en-suite. I've knocked and called through the door but still no response, so looks like I'm going to see my sister naked for the first time in at least a couple of years.

'Rosie, this is your last warning, I'm coming in… I mean it!'

I gingerly push open the door and stick a hand in so she can see that I mean it. No shouting. Hmm, she's playing hardball then. I slide in through the smallest gap I can make in the doorway.

'No, no, no!! What are you doing?!'

Rosie is completely submerged in the bath looking lifeless, her eyes bulged open and her cheeks don't look full of air, nor are there bubbles coming from her nose. I rush to the bath almost slipping on the wet floor and wrap my arms around her shoulders, pulling her into a sitting position. Thank goodness that she takes a large, spluttering breath as soon as she's out of the water.

'Eurgh, what are you doing, Poppy?! Get out!'

'Sorry, I won't bother saving your life next time then, I guess. Mum's home, you need to come down and talk to her now before Dad gets in.'

'I was relaxing in the bath, not dying. Get out, please, I'll be down in five.'

Rosie shoves me towards the door and I can't be bothered to argue because if this was what it looked like then I don't want to make her feel worse.

'Fine, hurry up then, kid.'

'You're a homo?'

'Mum, that's not the right word to use now!'

Daisy and I both practically shout at our mum. We may have only just found out our sister's secret but we will always defend her no matter what.

'Sorry, girls, Rosie I didn't meant to upset you, I am just so confused. I never thought I would be having this conversation, especially with you. You were always the one with all the boys after you growing up.'

Rosie flashes me and Daisy a smug smile at this, always wanting to be the centre of attention this one.

'I didn't know then, I thought I was just with the wrong guy, so I tried another, and another, thinking I would find the right one. The closest I came was when I dated Steve, remember the one who used to read the girly magazines and took more time to get ready in the mornings than me? We had things in common, he liked the same shows as me, he knew what clothes I should wear to show off my shape, he could tell me what lipstick would suit my outfit.'

'Steve was gay!'

Rosie rolls her eyes at me before continuing.

'Yes, I know that now, I dumped him because I thought he was gay, but it made me realise that I was too. He was the only boyfriend I had that I didn't feel a complete fraud with. After Steve, I swore off men, remember?'

We all nod unanimously. I definitely remember thinking it would never happen.

'Well… I wasn't joking. He was my last boyfriend. I joined a dating site and went on a few dates before I met Fiona. Dating was suddenly fun and exciting and romantic, nothing like I had ever experienced before. I was pretty sure by then that I liked women, then I met Fiona and it was love at first sight. I was desperate for you all to meet her but I was so scared that you wouldn't approve or you would treat me differently, so I introduced her as a friend. It was just a couple of weeks later that I met Travis, as a friend, and we got talking and came up with a way of keeping everyone happy.'

I hear a sniff to the side of me and reach out to take my mum's hand with a sympathetic smile, as Rosie sits quietly now, inspecting her nails and refusing to make eye contact with anyone. Daisy is staring off into the distance; clearly hearing this whole thing for the second time is less exciting.

'You would have married a man you don't love just to keep me and your dad happy?'

Mum's voice is wavering as she says this and I can't tell if she is sad or angry but the hairs on the back of my neck are on end. Growing up, I was the one who got this tone from our mum the most and just like now it was impossible to know if she was about to shout or if she was disappointed.

'Yes, I mean no, I don't actually know if I would have gone through with the wedding... Yes I would have. Oh, Mum, I just don't know what I'm doing with my life. I feel like I'm letting everyone down now and I have messed everything up. Poor Travis, and his mum, she really is so sweet. Dad is going to be so angry with me, isn't he?'

Rosie starts sobbing. Instantly Mum, Daisy and I are at her side. Mum has pulled Rosie away from the kitchen table and wrapped her arms around her with me and Daisy on either side. We stay like this, feeling the deep shuddering sobs coming from the youngest family member, until our dad walks in.

'What's happened? Has Travis done something? Right, I'm going over to his work!'

Dad is out of the door before Rosie can even lift her head from Mum's chest to say anything.

'Do you want me to tell him for you, sweetheart, or do you want to talk to him yourself?'

'Will you tell him, Mum? I can't say this whole thing again.'

'Righto, stay here then.'

Mum gives Rosie a tender kiss on her forehead and rushes out of the kitchen door, calling after our dad. For a moment the three of us sit silently, no one knowing what to say or do, then suddenly we hear our dad's raised voice. He's shouting at Mum about someone called Beverly. The car door slams, sounding as loud as a gunshot, then the car tires crunch on the gravel of our driveway. Rosie wails uncontrollably; she's always been the biggest daddy's girl and wants nothing more than to make him proud. Unlike me and Daisy, who seem to compete against each other, but mostly do what we want and screw the consequences.

'Dad just needs a little time. Shall we have another cup of tea? Maybe I could make us a cake, it's so rare that I have all my girls home for the night.'

'Do you hate me, Mum?'

'Rosie, no matter what, I could never hate you, any of you! I am so proud of all of you and any decisions you make or the life you lead. Don't ever feel you have to be something else for me and Dad. He may need a couple of rounds of golf to think things through but he will support you no matter what. Shall we make fairy cakes together like we used to when you were all little?'

Rosie nods and that is the end of that conversation.

'That's Dad's car!'

Daisy is next to the window looking out for Dad. He's been gone for hours and we have been getting worried.

Rosie bounces out of her seat and goes to intercept him as he heads towards the stairs.

'Dad?'

He looks at her, his eyes tinged red either from tears or alcohol; hopefully the first because he drove home. They stand staring at each other as we watch them like some sort of reality show. Mum clears her throat and it seems to kickstart Dad.

'I have a sister called Beverly. She was much older than me and I remember when I was a young lad she told our dad that she was queer. It was a different time back then. Your granddad… he… beat her and told her she was no longer his daughter. I didn't understand any of it at the time, all I knew was that my dad didn't approve, so I've grown up thinking that's normal. I haven't seen my sister since that day when she left our family home covered in blood, her and your gran crying. I still have nightmares sometimes. I will not be like that man. Rosie, this has obviously been a complete shock to me and it will take time for me to come to terms with it.

I hope you understand if I would rather not hear about your relationship with a lady friend for some time and I apologise in advance for any mistakes I make along the way, it's not something I want to be discussing, but…'

My dad pauses and rubs the back of his hand across his eyes.

'I love you girls more than life itself, don't be scared to talk to me about anything.'

The three of us surround our big strong father and hug him tightly. He lets out a small sob as he wraps his protective arms around us.

'I still want some wedding cake, even though the big day is being cancelled. Your mum has had me on a diet for the wedding.'

'We made fairy cakes whilst you were out, Dad.'

'I love you girls, now take me to the cake!'

★★★

Laura Lawrence is a self-published author with her ebooks available on Amazon here:

https://www.amazon.co.uk/kindle-dbs/author/ref=dbs_P_W_auth?_encoding=UTF8&author=Laura%20Lawrence&searchAlias=digital-text&asin=B00D99WYTE

She lives in Somerset and when she's not writing she is

looking after two of the most talkative children in the world, spending time with her husband and trying to sneak more pets or plants into the house. Laura dreams of having her own home library and is gradually filling her new house with books to make this happen!

REFLECTED

D. Wells

The ornate gilded mirror stood proudly on the wall. It had stood there for years. It was not an obvious place for a mirror, hidden in a darkened section of hallway and slightly too high to comfortably view yourself. It was a mirror that looked beautiful but was rarely used.

Pippa had, for years, been grateful for the excuse not to. The only other mirror in the house was the one on the backside of her wardrobe door, purposely kept closed so she wouldn't have to contemplate all the decades that had passed across her features. The spread that had crept across her body, post-children and now post-menopause. The mirror could be a cruel reminder of time passed and she happily avoided its unrelenting honesty.

However, that morning, something felt different. The recent surgery, the prolonged stay in hospital and the loss of her hair, which only now was growing back in determined stumps, all contributed to the heavy charge of change in the air. She had faced the hardest chapter of her life. She'd seen first-hand, had *felt* the devastation of a failing body. She was no longer afraid, or shy, or concerned to appraise her appearance.

The mirror seemed a trivial adversary these days.

She approached the oval frame, vintage in design and in age too. For once a natural sunlight cast a flattering golden light through the hallway and lifted the darkness away at the edges. Her hand reached out to the frame, lightly brushing its cold metallic surface, before she manoeuvred her body to face it square on.

She lifted her head slowly and looked. Her skin was pale, but not sickly like it had been only months before, when she had cringed as she stared into the tiny pocket mirror usually kept in her toiletry bag. She was still in hospital then and curiosity led her to take a quick peek. Her skin was grey, haggard looking, her hair almost entirely absent. It had been a devastating glimpse.

Now, her complexion looked fresher. It looked healthier. Yet the telltale signs were there; pale, wrinkled with age, dark shadows below each eye. But Pippa wasn't unpleased. She knew she'd looked worse.

Tufts of honey-coloured hair framed her small head. The smattering of grey hadn't reappeared, but she knew they would eventually come. She wondered briefly if she may pull off the pixie look, her petite features lending themselves to the style. Her hair had always been long, except for a brief and regretted haircut – a bob, cut under her chin. But at all other times she had proudly kept her hair past her shoulders and spilling over her back. Even after having children, as her hair thinned and became brittle with age, she kept it long. She wasn't as heartbroken by its recent loss as she imagined she would be. That revelation surprised her even now.

Her small button nose wrinkled slightly as she tried a smile. The reflection showed her that, indeed, age and illness had caught up with her. As it did for all. Deep furrows crept upwards from the bridge of her nose to the middle of her forehead. Crow's feet spread backwards from her eyelids. The skin on her cheeks was losing its elasticity and thinning more each year. Her lips were still the softest pink buds and she felt a slight satisfaction that age hadn't robbed her of everything.

Pippa surveyed silently. Pulling a face of surprise, she marvelled at the way her expression warped her features to the point of barely looking recognisable. She winked at the mirror, observing another change. Her laughter lines grew deeper by the action, lifting her cheek muscles a fraction and amending the shape of her face from an elongated oval to a heart.

She laughed then. Partly to see how her face would adapt, partly amid the humour of a revelation. Liking what she saw, not feeling embarrassed or ashamed by her ageing features, her body began to relax, began to lighten. Her countenance changed. With all she had been through, she was no longer fearful of growing old.

All those years wasted, not wanting to peer into the reflective surface, unsure of how she might feel at the sight of the woman staring back at her. In reality, she was probably at her prime in those years, yet had not recognised it; even when carrying the stubborn weight from birthing two babies, the feeling of despair when nothing in her wardrobe seemed to fit. The heaviness of being tired, of having no time or energy to pull herself together, to make a difference, to lose the weight that she had allowed to burden and depress her thoughts.

Perhaps she had listened too often to the accusing voice within, telling her she was no longer attractive, that she was beyond beauty and society's interpretation of it. She should have ignored her inner doubts, she realised, but hindsight always brought with it an unwanted and uncomfortable clarity.

Pippa ran her slightly shaking hand over her short hair and pointed her chin upwards in a small act of defiance. Then she tilted her face downwards again, almost nodding to the mirror and accepting its appraisal of her.

She considered the mirror itself then. It was wasted in this space, hidden in the half light between the lounge and the kitchen. She vaguely remembered times when she'd even bobbed her head low, on the days she felt least confident, on her way to the kitchen to cook dinner or return to the lounge with a piping cup of coffee, not wanting to even witness the briefest of glances across its smooth surface.

That would need to change, she reasoned. Why shouldn't she contemplate her appearance and indeed her recovery? Perhaps, even, she could feel more comfortable by the advancing years, revel in the new signs across her features of the years turning golden and, hopefully, of wisdom replacing folly.

It would be a new chance. A new phase of life. A time where she could walk past the relocated mirror, give a confident smile in its direction, a fluff of her newly grown hair, perhaps even a puckered and playful grin directly into its exterior.

Pippa stood back and smiled determinedly. She nodded again, confident in her decision. Now was the time to give it centre stage. Not just the mirror, but also herself. Years of being shy of each other would change. Now they could both stand in the light; prominent, unashamed and unafraid of the truth reflected in each of them.

***

D. Wells is an indie author of UpLit fiction. She has published several short stories and a full-length novel *6 Caledon Street*. She is married, has three young children and resides in East Anglia, UK. You can find her on all major social media sites and can browse her books at:

https://www.amazon.com/author/d.wells

OBLIVION

Laura Bland

It wasn't the best day I'd had, but then it also wasn't the worst, so at least I had that to be thankful for. In fact, as I looked around me and took in the scenes of devastation and destruction, I felt a giggle start to bubble up inside of me. I tried as hard as I could to supress it, but it was no use. Before I knew it, the giggle had escaped and had grown to be a full-sized belly laugh. I knew that I was on the verge of becoming hysterical but there was nothing I could do, it was no longer tears of laughter rolling down my cheeks.

How had so much happened in such a short space of time? And how on earth was I going to explain this away?

"Miss, you need to come with us, please. Miss, can you please stand up and come with us? We need to move away from the fire. Miss!" A man was shouting right by me, but I barely even registered the sound of his voice.

I could hear sirens and hurried footsteps all around me but it seemed so distant and so far away.

"Miss, if you don't stand up and come with us, I'm going to have to make you."

It was only when two hands grabbed hold of me roughly that I realised he had been talking to me. Everything seemed to be in a fog and it wasn't just the smoke from the fire. It was as if I were being spoken to from a long way off; I could barely make sense of the voices. What was going on? How had this happened? What would happen to me now? Where was Daisy?

There were hands on my upper arms now, they were dragging me to my feet and propelling me across the yard. I moved my head slowly from side to side as we went. It was horrific, barely anything had been left untouched by the blaze. I could hear more sirens approaching but it was hard to tell if they were already here or still a long way off, that fog that had gripped me just wouldn't let go.

"Here, quick, bring her to me. She's bleeding. I'll need to check her over."

This time it was a female voice but I had no idea where it was coming from; each step we took was like walking through quicksand and my head was getting so heavy it was hard to hold it up.

"Quick, grab her before she…"

When I woke up, the light overhead was too bright and it hurt my eyes; in fact, everywhere hurt, so I let myself quickly retreat back into oblivion.

"We need to speak to her. There are a lot of questions that we need answering. We need to find out what happened. When can we interview her?" There was that voice again, the man with the rough hands.

"She hasn't remained conscious yet for more than a few seconds at a time. But beyond a few cuts and bruises, there is no real sign of trauma, so we're not sure yet what's causing her to black out like this." Female this time, soft but firm. I had no idea who she was, but I already knew I liked her.

"But when will she be ready to talk?" There he was again – rough hands! What was going on? I must have been in hospital, that would explain the too bright lights and the crisp sheets I could feel against my skin, but why was I here? Why was it so hard to remember anything or to move? Why did my whole body hurt so much?

"I really don't know what to tell you, Detective Robins. It's impossible to say how long she might be like this. Once she wakes and is ready to talk, I'll have a nurse call you, but for now you will need to leave."

Well now I had a name at least. I heard heavy footsteps followed by a door opening and closing; I assumed the detective must have left. I tried again to open my eyes but they just wouldn't respond. My whole body seemed to have turned against me, so I gave in to the black oblivion again.

The next time I woke, it wasn't so painful and the fog had lifted a little, I was able to push myself up and look around the room. I was met with stark white walls, a room with no love, no personality, no warmth. I tried to get up but a wave of pain and nausea hit me, forcing me back down. I waited for the nausea to pass and then slowly sat up again. I was more cautious this time, moving as slowly as I could, not wanting to push myself too hard.

"Ah, you're finally awake and up. That's a good sign; you've been in and out of consciousness for the last forty-eight hours. I'm Dr Sloan, I've been looking after you since you were brought in on Saturday. You've had us worried, so it's good to see you awake." Dr Sloan had a kind open face, she wore her hair pulled back into a high ponytail, and a small pair of glasses perched on her nose. I guessed she was probably around fifty, though it was hard to tell.

"I've been here two days?" How had I lost that much time? "I need to go. I need to get out of here. I need to find Daisy, she was at the stables, there was a fire, I need to find her." I pulled back the sheet and started to swing my legs out of the bed but the doctor came rushing over.

She placed her hands on my shoulders and pushed me back onto the bed. I knew she was trying to be gentle but searing pain shot through my left shoulder and the room began to go dark again. I think she sensed how much she was hurting me, as she snatched her hands away. "I'm sorry, Callie, but you need to stay here, you're in no fit state to go anywhere right now and the police need to speak with you." She started to retreat across the room. "Please stay here and don't try to get out of bed again. You're not strong enough right now and we need to run more tests." There was a note of urgency to her voice now and, although I desperately wanted to leave, I knew that I didn't have the energy; even if I did make it out of the bed, I wouldn't make it across the room, let alone out of the hospital.

I gave back into the oblivion and let the darkness carry me away.

I woke later but I had no idea how much time had passed. The fog had lifted further from my mind and the light didn't hurt my eyes so much. This time when I tried to sit up I couldn't, but not because I was too weak or it hurt too much. When I tried to move, I found I'd been strapped to the bed, both my wrists and ankles were tied down. What the hell was going on? Why was I tied down like a common criminal or a crazy person? I did the only thing that I could, I started to shout.

"Help, help, help me. Is anyone there? HELP!"

Dr Sloan returned to my room. "Okay, Callie, you can stop shouting now, just calm down. I need you to calm down and stop this shouting." Her voice was so quiet but firm; she was clearly trying to reason with me but I just carried on shouting. "This isn't going to help. You're going to tire yourself out again. Calm down or I'll have to call for help and then it will be out of my hands." That got my attention and shut me up. She was talking to me as though it was perfectly reasonable that I was tied up, or had she just not even noticed?

"Why am I tied up?" I almost shouted the words at her I was getting so cross. I needed answers and I needed to get out of here. I still had no idea where Daisy was or if she was okay. "Please, just tell me what's going on, why have I been tied up?" It came out on a sigh, almost a sob really, I was so confused, I just wanted to know what was happening.

"You're not tied up, at least not in the way you think." Finally, she was talking to me. "We had to restrain you to prevent you from hurting yourself. When you blacked out again you must have started to have nightmares, you were thrashing around and tearing at your face. We sedated you and restrained you so you couldn't hurt yourself again." There it was, that all too reasonable voice again.

She must have been lying, that sounded crazy. I didn't remember any of that.

Doctor Sloan came over to the bed and released my right hand from the restraint. "Here, take this," she said as she passed me a small mirror. I held it up to my face and just like she had said there were fresh scratch marks across my cheek. There were dark circles around my eyes and my normally glossy brown hair was tangled and clumped around my head. I dropped the mirror back down as a single tear escaped and rolled down my cheek.

Silently, Doctor Sloan moved around the bed and removed the remaining restraints. She started to speak again as she came back around to where she had started. "I've had to inform Detective Robins that you're awake, so it won't be long before he is here to talk to you." She paused, as though she were struggling for words. "There are a lot of people with a lot of questions and right now you're the only one that might have the answers." She pushed her hands deep into the pockets of her white coat and looked down at the floor, then she turned away and was gone and I was alone again in that stark white room.

She had been right, though, I wasn't alone for long before the detective arrived. I heard him before I saw him, his voice was unmistakeable. I was immediately transported back to that night; I could smell the smoke and feel the heat of the fire on my skin; I couldn't breathe, the room started to turn black. It was like I was being smothered.

The voice of Detective Robins snapped me back to reality. "Callie, my name is Detective Robins. Do you remember me? I helped pull you out of the rubble on Saturday. This is my colleague, Detective Waters." He gestured to the woman standing behind him as he said this. She was tall with a pretty face and long blonde hair. She had a pen and notebook in her hand already and looked like she was poised to write down anything I said.

"Hi." It was all I could manage. I wasn't really sure yet exactly what had happened or how bad things were, so I didn't know what else to say.

"Callie, we need to ask you some questions about what happened last Saturday. Do you feel up to talking to us?" This time it was Detective Waters talking; she was looking at me so intently that I had to look away. I noticed Detective Robins moving across the room; there was a chair in the far corner. I hadn't noticed it before but he grabbed hold of it and dragged it across the floor till it was right up by the side of my bed. I noticed then just how big his hands were and remembered the rough feel of them on my arms as he had dragged me away from the danger last week. Waters cleared her throat and snapped my attention back to her.

"Sorry, yes," I stammered. "I can answer some questions but I'm not sure how much I can help." I was nervous and I knew it showed; I couldn't stop fiddling with the seam of the bedsheet, it was like a nervous tick that I had all of a sudden picked up. I smoothed the sheet back down and laced my fingers together across my lap in a bid to keep my hands still.

"Do you know where Daisy is? Have you found Daisy? Is she okay?" I looked from one to the other as I threw the questions at them but neither of them spoke; they exchanged a look and I thought Waters nodded at Robins, but still neither of them answered me. Why were they just ignoring me? Did they already know where Daisy was?

"What were you doing at the stables so late on Saturday? How did the fire get started?" It was Robins again this time doing the talking; it was like they were playing tennis, taking it in turns to hit questions at me. It was already starting to hurt my head. I didn't know who to focus on.

"Wait," I snapped at them as I held both my hands up and closed my eyes. "I can't think, give me time to breathe."

"Time to breathe or time to come up with some convincing lies?" This time it was Waters. She was standing now, leaning against the doorframe, her arms folded across her chest and a look on her face that clearly said she wasn't going to believe a word of what I said. I turned to Robins; maybe he would be more reasonable, but I couldn't read him at all. He sat on the old blue chair that he had dragged across the room and just watched me.

Before they could fire any more questions at me, Doctor Sloan came back into the room. "Sorry guys, but I'm going to have to ask you to step out for a few minutes. I need to do a check on Callie's vitals. Why don't you go grab a coffee and come back in ten minutes?"

I could see they were reluctant to leave but slowly they did as they were told and I was alone with the doctor again. "How are you doing? I hope they're not being too hard on you." As she talked, she was applying a cuff to my upper arm. I guessed she was checking my blood pressure but she never explained anything. After looking at the monitors around me, she started noting things down on a chart that was hanging on the end of my bed. I had no idea if what she was seeing was good or bad.

Before I knew it, Robins and Waters were back and they looked like they wanted those answers. They settled back into their previous positions, Robins in the old chair by my bed and Waters over by the door. Has she chosen to stand there in case I tried to make a run for it? "I'm not even sure my legs will work right now. I'm not about to go running off, you know." Robins just shrugged at me, but she didn't move away from her post. The only thing she did do was get her notebook back out.

"So, you were about to tell us what had happened..."

"Wait, before I tell you anything, I want to know where Daisy is, did you find her? Is she okay?" I prayed they would actually answer me this time, but I was just met with stony silence again.

Robins sat forward in the chair. "Callie, I'm not sure that you realise just how serious things are for you right now. When we found you last Saturday the stables had all but burnt down around you. All fifteen horses missing, some of them worth hundreds of thousands of pounds, not to mention the value of the equipment that was destroyed and the stables itself." He leant back in his chair and ran one hand through his hair before he continued. "Right now, unless you can give us some answers, you're our only suspect in what looks like an arson. If you're charged with this, you could end up in prison. Do you understand what I'm saying?"

Prison... but none of this was my fault. I hadn't even planned to go to the stables that night, it was purely by chance that I happened to be there. But then everything went so wrong, and now here I was stuck in hospital and being threatened with prison. How had my life turned to this so fast?

Less than a week ago my biggest issue was deciding what to have for tea and now here I was in a hospital bed being questioned by the police, I had no idea where Daisy was, all the horses were gone and the stables had burnt down. It was a good job Mum and Dad weren't around to see how things had changed, they would be horrified. It had taken them decades to build up the business. When I had inherited it, I wasn't sure if I would run it or sell it but I had never wanted anything like this to happen.

I took a deep breath and started to speak. "It all started last Wednesday. Daisy came home and told me she was eloping with Adam. They barely knew each other but they were planning to run off and get married! I knew he was no good for her. But she was so stubborn she just wouldn't listen to me."

My voice trailed off as I got drawn into a memory: one of the last times we had spoken had been a huge fight. *"Daisy, he's no good. He's just after your money. Why can't you see that?"* I hadn't meant to raise my voice but I couldn't help it.

"You don't understand, you never will. You haven't been in love, not the way that we are. He's the best thing to happen to me." And with that, Daisy had stormed off. My first instinct was to chase after her but something made me hold back. I regretted that decision almost immediately.

That was the day. The worst day of my life. Wednesday. The day it all started to unfold. The day I lost Daisy, possibly forever.

For the next few days, I saw and heard nothing of Daisy. I checked all of her normal hangouts and called all of her friends but they hadn't seen her either. I was already going out of my mind with worry and then as I was driving home on Saturday night, I caught a glimpse of her. I was driving past the stables on my way home and all of a sudden there she was. She was running across the yard and, although I could barely see her, I could sense that she was afraid. She was running from something, or someone. I leapt from the car and started racing after her trying to catch up to her. And that's when the horrors of Saturday night started to unfold…

★★★

Laura Bland is based in Leicestershire UK, with her partner and their gorgeous daughter. Laura has always loved to read and finds joy in escaping into a good book, so being able to give this to others is a privilege. Laura owns and runs Laura B Fitness Coach and Mentor providing online fitness solutions to women across the globe:

www.laurab-fitnessmentor.com

A BIRTHDAY TO REMEMBER

Leah Strachan

Bang! That's the sound of my two twin siblings, Jade and Jimmy, frantically running around the living room popping my birthday balloons. Jade is screaming at an unbothered Jimmy who is trying to balance a big, blue balloon on his nose. I grab a slice of my birthday cake and run upstairs; yes, if you haven't guessed, it is my birthday! However, I'm stuck inside and can't go out.

Let me explain. It was five o'clock last Monday, my mum, dad, brother and I were all gathered around the small TV in my room. The twins were in the garden running around because Dad didn't want them worrying about the big C word… Coronavirus. My dad, Peter, is very overprotective; he cares a lot about what we know and how we know it.

My mum, Sandra, on the other hand doesn't mind us knowing, as long as it's from a reliable source. Although, her version of a 'reliable source' is a fake news report her friend Jan put on her WhatsApp group chat.

The news camera panned over to Boris Johnson

sitting at a desk, who started telling us the updates. I freeze as he orders us to stay inside at all times unless for certain vital reasons. My mum squeezes my hand as she knows this is a massive change for me. Suddenly, a wave of reality hit me. Not only am I not doing my GCSEs but my sixteenth birthday is ruined too! Everything I'd planned can no longer happen. I'm acting as though I had planned a holiday to Majorca; what I'd actually planned was to go to the theatre then visit my favourite Italian restaurant. Not as good as Majorca, but I was looking forward to it nonetheless. Everybody plodded to their bedrooms sluggishly whilst fearing the unknown of what else was to happen. Well, that and also dreading spending weeks at home with the whole family, it's enough to send shivers down your spine!

The next morning, well afternoon (why should I wake up early when I've got nothing to do?) I walked downstairs to get some breakfast. I went and sat with Jade at the dining table. She was doing her year four schoolwork. I looked over to her sheet, and read her answers. The question was "3 x 20 = 60, how do you know this?" Jade's answer was "because I have a brain." I silently laughed to myself and walked off so I didn't distract her. I grabbed my Coco Pops and went back up to bed to watch Netflix.

By the third day, I'd surprisingly got bored of staying in bed all day; I suggested to my mum that we go for a family walk as it was swelteringly sunny outside. The twins were wearing sandals and had thick white lines of sunscreen down their noses that glistened in the sun. To no one's surprise, my elder brother Jake decided to stay at home to play videogames. We had been walking for ten minutes when it suddenly became cooler and a freezing drop landed on my brow. Out of nowhere, a colossal flood of rain came pouring down onto us. We started sprinting back home, the twins' sandals flapping and squelching. Eventually, we stumbled through the door as Jake was in the kitchen grabbing a drink. "You look like a bunch of drowned rats!" he sniggered as I sulked off to my room.

The next day, I was awoken by my whole family – even Jake – standing over my bed looking down at me.

"Happy birthday!" they shouted in unison.

I looked over to my clock.

"Six o'clock?" I screamed. "SIX O' BLOODY CLOCK!"

Jade and Jimmy, who were jumping on my bed, swiftly got down and ran out of my room, followed by Jake and my parents.

When I finally woke up and went downstairs, I was greeted by Jade screaming about how it's her birthday. I, of course, tried to explain that in fact it is my birthday not hers but it was obviously no use.

The next thing I know, I'm looking down at a pair

of socks laid out on my lap, and not cute socks either. However, I did get a few good gifts such as clothes that I wanted but no longer need as I have nowhere to wear them as we're all grounded! Also, why does everybody feel the need to buy teenage girls bath stuff? I get it's an easy thing to buy as they're guaranteed to like it, but when you end up with a pile of body washes and a few bath bombs, I'm left thinking... *Do I smell?* Oh, and perfumes! It's like: happy birthday, here's some spray to cover up your foul smell! But despite this, I am very grateful for all of my gifts, honestly!

By lunchtime, I was sitting in my room watching YouTube. This was the most boring birthday ever. I couldn't blame anyone either, because none of this was their fault, it is what it is I suppose. The thought of going on a walk entered my mind then quickly left when I remembered what happened last time. I turned my computer off and went into Jake's room. On the way there, I saw Jade painting my dad's fingernails and Jimmy having a lightsaber fight with my mum. As I walked into his dark and musty room, Jake covered his headset's microphone and whispered, "What do you want?"

I gave him an innocent look to make him feel guilty for snapping, since it was my birthday after all. He shook his head, sighed, and reluctantly turned his PlayStation off.

"Do you want to come outside? It's sunny." I asked.

"Yes, I suppose, since I have to." He sulked.

We sat on the grass as we soaked in the sun and joked about life after quarantine. After a while, the rest of the family came out too. Me and Mum relaxed in the sun with a can of Fanta and some grapes whilst Dad, Jimmy, Jade and somehow even Jake played tig. A moment later, our neighbour came out into their garden. Then another neighbour came out, and another, and another until everybody was standing out in their gardens. "Boris wouldn't like this!" I sniggered.

"Why not?" queried Mum. "We're not near each other."

"Why is everyone suddenly outside, anyway?" I asked.

Suddenly it went silent.

I turned around to everybody staring at me, then they started singing!

"Happy birthday to you! Happy birthday to you! Happy birthday to Talia! Happy birthday to you!"

My face turned a brighter red with every word they sang. Then the clapping began and at this point I was as red as a tomato and wishing the ground would swallow me whole. Then it was silent again. I waved to everyone whilst giving my thanks as people placed gifts by my gate.

So yes, that was different, but definitely a birthday to remember.

★★★

Leah Strachan is a thirteen-year-old girl from Leicester. She's loved reading books from a young age and loves writing stories even more. Thank you for taking the time to read her story, I hope you enjoyed it! If you'd like to get in touch then you can do so via Fuzzy Flamingo: contact@fuzzyflamingo.co.uk

WILLOW TREES AND RAINBOWS

Alex Preston

She opened her eyes for the one hundredth time, but the darkness wouldn't shift. The walls were closing in, she could feel them now, the rough surface grating the skin on the soles of her feet. Something trapped the strands of her hair, ripping them out one by one. Her hands were jacked up against her chest and she could barely move. Her wrists were bound so tightly that her fingers bulged. She blinked frantically but it was hopeless, the outside was just as black as the insides of her eyelids, nothing but cold relentless darkness.

Everything felt slow and dizziness crept in, the box that Lexi found herself in began to spin. The tips of her fingers tingled, her lips burned and quickly the wildfire had spread across her entire body, drowning her. Goosebumps stood every single one of her hairs on end, her heart pounded in her chest and something crushed down on her ribcage, suffocating her. Unable to breathe, Lexi gasped for air, thrashing with every ounce of strength she could muster, but it was useless. Still she fought, her arms were heavy, but she punched and scratched at the box, tearing her nails to shreds, blood streaming from her knuckles.

Lexi never gave up. Her eyes were bulging, and her time was running out, the noose around her neck tightened, choking her. She tried to scream but nothing came out.

Salty bile stung the back of her throat but still she tried to scream again; nothing, not a sound, no one was coming for her. This was it.

Her brain fogged over, nothing made sense, everything felt foreign to her and the air was like treacle. Shaking uncontrollably, she tried one last time to save herself. Sweat dripped down her face, her eyes darted back and forth in search of something, anything that might help her.

Lexi was a fighter through and through and she was not giving up without a fight; she had survived worse. Scrambling in the darkness, she felt a pain soar through her thigh, something hard, cold and sharp jabbed at her side. She managed to wrangle her right arm free and grab it; this was it, this might just save her.

She wrangled to figure out what she had found but blood red smoke suddenly filled the space around her and set the box alight. Pain soared through her chest; it was too late, this was it, this was her last breath.

★

Lexi shot up in bed, wide-eyed and clutching her smoky quartz crystal in the palm of her right hand. "A nightmare, just another nightmare," she told herself.

Lexi had always been a fighter, a fierce protector but the world was different now, she was scared and confused. Life might not ever be the same and Lexi was mad about it, mad because she saw it coming and mad because she couldn't escape. Her world was a nightmare and even in her sleep she was plagued with the terror inside her own head.

Lexi grew up in the city, but she was made for living surrounded by fields and trees, the kind of woman who came to life in nature, it fed her soul. The energies of the moon spoke to her more than most; she didn't always understand them but her connection with the earth was special. People were an important part of Lexi's world, something she had only just really grasped, now that it had all been taken away from her.

The world was spinning out of control and Lexi wanted it to stop. She missed the bumble bees, missed seeing the stars in the sky, the smell of freshly roasted coffee and the buzz of people, but all that seemed like a convoluted distant dream.

The last thing Lexi could remember of normal life was pulling weeds from her vegetable patch with the sun beating down on her back. She remembered the soil underneath her fingernails and the green caterpillar she spotted while she was struggling with the sticky weeds. She yearned to be fighting with pigeons again; the old man on the back had been causing chaos feeding the wild birds for years and they wreaked havoc in Lexi's vegetable patch, it drove her crazy. They were gone now, along with the old man, disappeared to God knows where like the rest of the town and Lexi would do anything to be locking horns with a bloody pigeon again.

Instead of tucking into freshly plucked homegrown vegetables, wandering barefoot around stone circles or writing blogs about it all, Lexi was on her bed panting, dripping with sweat, wide-eyed and alone. Gradually she came round a little, just enough to catch her breath. Her room was pin-drop silent, no cars rushed by outside, no birds tweeted. It was uncomfortable, and the silence haunted her. Crystal in hand, she took a deep breath. Lexi needed to purge the nightmare. Deep breaths in through her nose and out through her mouth, she was a pro at meditation now, she had practiced enough. With each breath in she imagined a bright light creeping in through her window and filling her body, cleansing every cell. On each breath out the blackness left her; after a few minutes, Lexi felt calm again. She grabbed her journal, scribbled down her dream and dragged herself out of bed.

Sitting at the table, she stared into her disappointing instant coffee, contemplating the day ahead. She had to leave the house and collect supplies. Her cupboards were depressingly bare and the vegetables in her garden getting smaller by the day. She feared these trips would become frequent, it filled her with dread. She felt like an animal locked away in her house day after day but at the same time the thought of going out there into the dead world depressed her just as much; she couldn't win but at least leaving broke the monotony of staring at the same four walls.

She made a list, knowing that she wouldn't get any of it but it made her feel better, in control and prepared; somehow the normality helped. The trip wouldn't be normal, there was nothing normal about any of it. At one point it would have excited her to leave the house, as it meant an opportunity. She had hopes that the devastation around them would bring people together, that she would go out and find wonderful people to talk to. She longed for a hug or a smile, something meaningful, but people had changed and she wasn't even sure they could see her. Neighbours had moved on and those that were left seemed to forget what it was to be human, they had withdrawn and lost the ability to experience emotion, like an infection, everyone else seemed to just exist. She hated it.

Downing her crappy coffee, she threw on some clothes and headed out of the door.

Outside, wandering slowly, Lexi hung her head at the barren wasteland that had replaced the green grass that once lined the path; no flowers, no people, no squirrels, just lifeless landscapes littered with plastic bottles, thrown away face masks, crisps packets and cigarette ends.

"Where does it all come from?" she asked herself. It broke her heart. She had tried so hard to help people understand the damage their consumerism was causing the planet and once upon a time she even thought that people were listening. She had really thought they would wake up to their selfishness, but it was too late, and all of this was our fault; humans had caused the end of the world.

She took her time walking along the deserted rubbish-strewn roads, taking in every disgraceful sight, she wanted to remember it so that if the world ever did recover she wouldn't forget the sickness and maybe, just maybe, she could stop it from happening again.

The sky was a grey blanket of thick heavy smog but somewhere on the other side of it was the sun and it was on fire; it was getting hotter as each day passed, scorching the earth, punishing us for killing it. Lexi was soaked in sweat and fought the urge to pull off the mask covering her face. She had made that mistake before and she did not want to revisit the hellish cough that almost took her out. It took everything to fight against the instinct.

Eventually she made it to the ration point just outside of a deserted supermarket. Makeshift tents covered small tables, which were manned by guards packing boxes and directing the crowds.

Along her journey, she had not seen another living soul, but here hundreds were gathered. She couldn't work out where they all hid, she had never seen so many people. They were different now, Lexi could feel it, their energy was odd. She couldn't quite put her finger on it, but they shuffled along, emotionless, uninterested and withdrawn like clones. Swarms of robotic people queued in perfectly straight lines to collect boxes of tinned peaches, beans and medications. The numbers got bigger with every visit and Lexi wondered how long the government aid might last. She wondered whether the government was still actually the government and what would happen when the food ran out.

The supermarkets had closed almost immediately, ransacked of all their goods and supply chains lost. The small town shops were next, pillaged by people for miles around panicking and stockpiling anything they could get their hands on, supposedly to give them a sense of safety. She imagined the amount of food wasted and the chemicals it poured into the atmosphere. It disappointed her that it had been allowed to happen, the irreversible damage it had done, and now people might actually starve to death.

Lexi joined the smallest queue she could find and stood watching people standing in line, no one speaking, not even turning their heads to acknowledge each other. The queues were long and still, nothing seemed to move, yet no one seemed to be bothered, they just stood there. The guards handed out box after box and not one person uttered a word of thanks.

She stood still for so long she had to fight her eyes from closing, then, just as she thought she might fall asleep standing upright, she heard something, did someone just speak? Where did it come from? For a second, Lexi thought she might have imagined it but then she saw him. Ahead of her, someone moved, his arms up in the air, he was yelling. She hadn't heard a person speak in weeks and the noised echoed in her ears. Looking around, no one else seemed to move, no one reacted to the man's yells but Lexi. She couldn't quite make out the words but somehow the voice seemed familiar. She didn't dare move from her spot in the queue, so she watched him for a second, throwing his arms in the air, gesturing at those in front. Hands on his hips now, he growled in frustration and then she clocked it. His tattoo. On the back of his arm was a willow tree and she recognised it instantly.

She remembered the day she first saw it at the Coffee Shack, it had reminded her of a willow tree that she used to have in her back yard as a child. There had been endless summer days lost sitting under that tree, playing in the sandpit. It was her favourite place; even so young, she felt its energy. For a second, she thought of her parents. She hadn't seen them in almost a year, she didn't know where they were or how they were. She had managed to speak to them on the phone occasionally but nowhere near enough. The phones were unreliable and the internet virtually non-existent.

"Cohen," she shouted. He stopped.

"COHEN!" Even louder this time.

He span around so fast he nearly lost his balance. Lexi couldn't make out his face because his mask covered it and his eyes were only just visible under his cap, but she knew, she could feel it, it was him. No one else moved an inch, they stayed perfectly still, staring ahead to the ration point; Lexi and Cohen seemed invisible to them. Cohen was next to collect his box. He grabbed it, remembered his manners and ran to Lexi. The box dropped next to Lexi's feet and Cohen bear hugged her. It was electric. Neither of them had touched anyone for as long as they could remember.

Cohen, in his past life, had been the barista at the Coffee Shack. The day they met, Lexi had been struggling with writer's block. It was difficult, sometimes, to be so full of ideas and passion, to see so clearly the desperate need to preserve our planet and treat it with respect but experience first-hand the inability of some to fathom the importance. Thoughts occasionally jumbled in Lexi's mind and the Coffee Shack was her retreat.

With a Tiger's eye gemstone in her pocket, she had thrown on her dungarees and scooped up her laptop. When she arrived at the Shack, she found her regular table, just by the window, nestled away in the corner, so set down her laptop and headed over to the counter. Cohen had just started his first shift and Lexi's order had been a little too hipster for him to cope with.

"Fair Trade, oat milk, dairy-free mocha with a shot of caramel syrup," she chirped.

Cohen gave it a good go but didn't quite master it. Lexi felt a little bad, so made a point to be friendly. She told him about the willow tree in her garden and how the willow symbolised strength and survival. He seemed to appreciate it and since then they had become friendly and Cohen would often spend his lunch break at Lexi's table chatting away.

Right now, here in this world it was surreal, Lexi couldn't quite believe it was him.

They chatted as Lexi waited for her ration box and, for the first time since it all began, she felt the warm fuzziness of happiness. As Lexi reached the collection point, she heard the guards say that's it. Behind her were lines twenty deep.

"That's it?" she asked the younger one of the three.

"Yes, we have one more shipment tomorrow but that's it," he said quietly.

"What about all these people, what happens to them?"

"They are all dead inside anyway."

Lexi and Cohen walked away in disbelief, unsure of what to say now or how to process the news. Lexi cried, she couldn't control it, it kept coming and she was hysterical.

"Here, come with me," Cohen said, grabbing her hand.

Eventually the tears stopped rolling long enough for Lexi to recognise where she was; the Shack. Cohen had been hiding out there. The owners had asked him to look after the place at the beginning of it all, but he hadn't heard from them since. They walked past tables and chairs that they had both sat on plenty of times before, through the staff room where Lexi noticed a mattress on the floor, down a dark and narrow hallway to a dirty white door. Cohen opened the door and inside were shelves stacked with tins of food, water, coffee, medicines and all sorts of other things left over from the Shack's supplies. Cohen had been saving it, meticulously arranging it and counting it. He had known that one day the food would run out.

Nothing between them was discussed, they both instinctively knew what they had to do. Loading every bag and box they could find, they prepared around fifty boxes of emergency supplies. By the time they had finished, the day had gone, it was pitch black and Lexi, usually dreading her bed, couldn't wait to lie down on the mattress and fall asleep.

Cohen had made himself at home in the staff room, the mattress for a makeshift bed was pushed up against the wall, lockers above where his head would rest were lined with dainty fairy lights and a small wooden crate overturned had a lamp perched on top. Scattered across the floor were piles of books, some Lexi recognised, his clothes were folded neatly over the back of a chair tucked away in the corner. It was small but felt cosy and Lexi felt safe there.

"You take the bed," he gestured towards the mattress.

"What about you?" Lexi asked.

"It's cool, I'll take the sofa in the shop."

"No, please don't do that, I don't mind, there is enough room for both of us!"

"Are you sure? I really don't mind; the sofa is fine."

"No, please, thank you, but no, it's okay. I have hardly seen another walking talking human for ages, it will be nice, please?"

"Okay, sure thing." He smiled back at her.

Neither bothered to undress; they barely had the energy to take off their shoes. Lexi climbed in and shuffled over to the edge to make room for Cohen. After a few moments of laying in silence, Lexi said, "Thank you."

"For what?" Cohen replied.

"Turning up, when I needed you to. I was heading down one big rabbit hole and who knows where I would have ended up, like one of the zombies probably."

He chuckled a little, turned to her, wrapped her in his arms and whispered, "You weren't the only one." Within minutes, both were fast asleep, exhausted from the day.

There were no lights in the staff room and no way to tell what time of day it was. Cohen lay there, staring at the ceiling, counting tiles until Lexi finally woke up.

"Coffee?" he asked.

"Yes!" she replied, rubbing her eyes. Cohen disappeared down the corridor towards the Shack. Lexi kicked off the covers and realised there had been no nightmares, not one single horrific thought had interrupted her sleep. It confused her a little as she wandered off in search of coffee.

Standing in the corner of the Shack, Lexi noticed all but one of the tables had chairs piled on top of them. All except her table, in the corner by the window.

"Sit down." A voice came from behind the counter.

Cohen appeared with two mugs of coffee and placed them on the table in front of her.

"One Fair Trade, oat milk, dairy-free mocha with a shot of caramel syrup, madame."

"Thank you," Lexi giggled.

She wrapped both hands around the mug and hugged it close to her chest. He wasn't joking! Fern leaf coffee art adorned the top of the mug, it smelt AMAZING, every sip set her taste buds on fire; she had never enjoyed a coffee as much as she did right now.

Lexi felt the energy shift, it lifted a little, seemed brighter and airier. Maybe it was her coffee, but a light caught her eye; it was almost like sunshine creeping through the smog. It didn't last long and soon she was thinking about the people who would be lining up at the ration point expecting a lifeline, food to feed them. She couldn't allow herself to think of the children that would starve and the suffering that would follow if no more food came.

They finished their coffee and loaded parcels into cages that had once housed cardboard for recycling. They pushed the rattling cages along the road. They were heavy and punishing. Neither had any idea what time of day it was but the heat was so incredible it must have been at least midday by the time they arrived at the ration point.

Rows and rows of people stood in perfectly-formed lines, motionless and waiting their turn. It was silent and the noise of the cages rang through the air; no one flinched. A voice came from the other end of the car park, it was one of guards.

"We are out!" he shouted.

Then another, this time closer. "Us too, nothing left."

One by one each station declared they were empty, yet no one moved, no one seemed to hear them. The guards looked at each other, all as confused as the next, unsure what to do. Still no one moved. They were rooted to the ground where they stood, glued to the spot. Lexi grabbed a box and shoved it into the hand of the man closest to her. For a second, he didn't move but slowly he lifted his head and looked straight into her eyes. Lexi thought he might speak, but nothing, he just took the box and walked away.

Cohen followed her lead and grabbed the hands of a woman in front of him. It seemed to startle her, she looked at her fingers and wiggled them in front of her face, as if she had only just discovered them. Cohen glanced over to Lexi who was already watching. "What the heck?" she mouthed in his direction. One by one, Lexi and Cohen handed out boxes. One by one the zombies appeared to wake up a little. Lexi came to a young girl, she put the box on the floor in front of her and put her hands on her shoulders. The girl jerked a little, her bright blue eyes wide.

"Are you okay?" Lexi asked. No reply. Lexi shook her gently and asked again.

"Hello, are you okay?" The young girl opened her mouth a little as if she was going to say something, but nothing came out. It was like she had forgotten how to talk. Slowly the girl came to life, lifting her arms and feet, looking at the box in front of them.

"Th... Th... Th... Thank you," she stuttered.

Lexi nearly fell over in disbelief. She shot a look to Cohen. One by one, people began to wake up from the trance they were in, moving fluidly, almost gracefully. They acknowledged each other, smiled and even hugged each other. Lexi stood crying, watching as the car park came to life, the energy had moved her, something had lifted, and it was easier to breathe. The sky was brighter somehow and then she saw it again, the light. This time it was bigger and colourful. Rainbows danced around them now, bouncing from one person to another and laughter echoed in the air. Something wet jumped across Lexi's hand, another trickled down her nose.

"Rain," she shouted, "COHEN IT'S RAIN!" Within seconds, the heavens opened, and rain drowned the ground, people clapped and cheered. This was it. The world was alive again. They had done it.

One single act of love and kindness had shifted the universe, human connection prevailed. The world was mending now. Lexi was mending now.

★★★

Alex Preston is from Nottingham, she is a mum of two girls. This is her first work of fiction although she has plans to write more in the future. As the co-owner of The Bottle Top, a zero waste and craft beer shop, her passion is the environment and supporting small businesses just like hers: www.thebottletopnotts.co.uk

THE GREAT GARDEN ESCAPE

Joanne Norwood

It was a typical school summer holiday morning. Simon and I had wolfed down the last of the Coco Pops topped with a soggy rusk. Sounds grim but you must try it, but only Farley's rusks will do!

So, what random craziness can we all get up to today? Being one of four has its perks during the school holidays, there's always someone to annoy or play with.

I could hear the distant hum of the motorway, birds chirping and that really annoying neighbour who seems to need a chainsaw for every job in the garden. I'd love to wrap it round his… erm, anyway.

I've decided den making is on today's agenda, so I've roped in my sister and we're off to raid the airing cupboard for den-making supplies.

Unfortunately for Mum, our supplies include all the best linen and the freshly washed sleeping bags. Bouncing down the stairs on our bums with arms stuffed with blankets, we are stopped in our tracks.

"No, no way – you are not taking all that outside.

I've just tidied that bloody cupboard up. Put it all back, you are not making a mess today!"

Devastated, life ruined. We march back up the stairs, shove it all in the cupboard and slope off to our bedroom totally deflated… and massively miffed! How could she be so cruel? All we wanted to do was bring every blanket, duvet cover and sleeping bag out and peg it up around the garden. What harm could it do? I'm not having this, I'm making a stand.

"That's it, we are moving out!" And with that, I began cooking up my master plan of how me, age ten, and my sister Emma, age eight, are leaving home and running away. We'll build shelters, live off the land and live in the shadows, never to be seen again.

Now we need to be sensible, we'll need some money. Our first mission, operation 'steal the building society books' out of Mum's admin cupboard. This was a squeaky old unit by the armchair full of receipts and letters in baskets. It also contained all our banking books and random pictures we had drawn for Mum over the years. Every now and then Mum would get it all out, pretend to be an accountant and then file it all away.

We will need food and water. I send Emma on a mission to raid all piggy banks and drawers. I knew my brother had a bag of change on his windowsill; not any more! We have well over two pounds now in spare change, winning!

We need spare clothes; one outfit should do it. I've picked my favourite coral t-shirt sporting a large image of Jasmin from Aladdin; won't stand out in that at all!

All set? So now how to escape out of the house without Mum catching us or one of my brothers grassing us up.

The garden seems the easiest option to slip away on our adventure.

There is a short concrete alleyway at the side of our house, at the end our tall, slightly wonky (another Dad bodge job) gate. I've decided we'll disguise our plan with a game of hopscotch in the alley. Our bags are hidden behind the cobweb-filled bins and it's game on.

Mum is on the phone chatting away to Karen, it's time to seize the moment. I can feel my heart beating out of my chest, my mouth is so dry I think I'll choke, but I grab Emma. "Run!"

We run so fast I feel like I'll take off at any minute; if one of us trips, the gravel rash will be horrendous! How Emma's milk bottle glasses didn't fly off, I'll never know.

What a rush! Wind in my hair, adrenaline pumping. We've done it, the adventure has begun. Two wild spirits roaming free forever.

I've got this great idea that we ditch a scarf en route then backtrack and run in the opposite direction. This would throw any detectives off the scent. I was born for this.

First stop is a couple of streets away, the local newsagents. We've used this shop for years. The old couple that run it are lovely but looked about a thousand years old. I send Emma in with our £3.50 to get essential supplies and I keep a lookout.

Emma comes out, smiling her head off looking super impressed with herself. What is in her blue carrier bag of delights?

"I got chewing gum to clean our teeth, some fizzy pop and sweets." Great, we'll one hundred percent survive now.

Off we go, ditch the scarf to cover our tracks, turn around and run towards the bridleway.

The clouds are starting to block the sun and the air is feeling a bit cooler. Emma is very quiet; did she even want to come? I notice her head twitching round like a meerkat. Every noise tightens the knot in our bellies.

Wandering around for what seemed like a lifetime we were discussing our sleeping arrangements for the night. Park bench? Den in the bushes? Hide in a shed? Ask a little old lady if we can stay over? We could carry out chores for a bed to sleep in.

Hmmm, I'm starting to feel a little unnerved now the sun is going down.

"Emma, why didn't we bring coats? Or blankets?" Or maybe the sleeping bags that had got us in this situation in the first place, I think.

"I'm cold," Emma mutters.

Looking around the housing estate we had bumbled into, things weren't looking so exciting. In fact, we were hit with the reality that we are two young girls completely lost and vulnerable.

Were the houses always this tall, towering over us, shadows getting bigger?

Anyone could pick us up, kidnap us, chop us up and eat us!

"I'm ringing Mum, we're going home."

With that the frantic search for a telephone box begins. I pop into a hardware store and ask to borrow their phone to call home, but I'm shooed away by the grumpy old goat behind the till.

Puffed out and desperate now for our adventure to end, we stand in the phone booth we've found, wide-eyed and shaky.

No money! Our little spend at the newsagents on sweets had left us skint.

Luckily, there's the reverse call charge option, so we give it a whirl… it's connecting, come on, Mum, you must have noticed we are missing now. Pick up the phone!

"Hi girls, where are you? We are sending a car to collect you. Stay exactly where you are." My guts have just fallen out of my ass, we are in deep trouble.

There was no question that the man that had taken our call was a police officer.

The wait for the police to collect us was unbearable, I could feel every tick of my watch.

The journey home was even worse. A dark-haired, soft-looking officer asked us a million questions. Why had we run away? Were we being abused? Did our parents beat us?

When I shakily explained that Mum hadn't let us

use the sleeping bags that morning to create dens, he didn't believe us. Surely there was more to it, a lifetime of abuse and terror at home. Two young girls desperate to escape.

Pulling up on the drive, Mum runs out and squeezes us. "You absolute idiots, I thought you had been snatched!"

What we didn't know was a car had been heard speeding off around the time we had gone out of the back gate. Mum had put two and two together: we must have been kidnapped.

For four hours, police had driven around Wigston, questioned neighbours and even searched our house and attic. The talk of the town.

My dad didn't speak to us for two weeks. It was all eyes on him while the police carried out their searches and investigations. Mum forced us to write letters of apology to everyone that went out hunting us down. The shame.

Fortunately, we only got as far as Whetstone. Things could have ended so differently.

Emma always blames me.

★★★

Joanne Norwood is a wife, mum of three strong-willed girls and a lover of music. She loves working with young people and runs the Queen Bee Youth Project in her village. Writing, violin and dancing are her passions.

Find her on social media: @queenbeeyouth

EDUCATING SOMEONE WITH AN EMPTY BRAIN

Charlotte Ryan

I'm Berni Inreb.

Just reached my teens, I have a love for discarded waste, power tools, nails, hammers…

Recycling bins have always sparked a passion within me. I am never just in one place, my imagination takes me all over the world on adventures.

Meet Mum.

Mum was Mum. She enjoyed gardening (Mum's idea of gardening anyway, i.e. sitting in our garden). My mum works as a cleaner for the National Health Service.

My story begins in the year 2020, I had just turned thirteen on the 9th of March. During the last few weeks everyone's life had changed quite considerably; well, my life had, but Mum's had not really.

No longer was I able to attend the lovely secondary school that I loathed, which was really a daily battle (with Mum) to get me there. I actually cheered and whooped out loud, much to the horror on my mum's face.

Sadly, we had never got on that well. I was a frustrated teenager stuck in a system that didn't fit me. I was misunderstood by everyone around me. We never saw eye to eye; I was that annoying little girl under her feet. Only I was not a little girl anymore, so I did my best to keep myself away from her feet!

Now if only Dad had been around, how different my life might have been…

The forgotten word D.A.D. said in silence, under muttered breaths. I was prohibited to mention those three letters, it was like he never existed. I knew from being a little girl at primary school that everyone had a dad.

I definitely did have a dad, but I had no idea what he looked like, where he lived, or why he wasn't here. No one had ever explained any of that to me, so instead I took to daydreaming often (that got me into a lot of trouble) of how I imagined things to be.

"I am just so bored, Mum, can't we go on holiday?"

"We cannot leave the house, Bernice, we are in a government lockdown."

"You mean I'm in lockdown, you still get to go to work."

Mum really didn't want to go to work. Deep down, she was worried about becoming unwell; who would look after me if she was ill?

"I've got itchy feet, Mum, I want to travel and explore the world. We have all this time now that I am not at school."

Thoughts entered my head: London to Big Ben, then off to the Pyramids of Egypt, then the Great Wall of China. I was not really paying attention to the words spilling out of my mother's mouth, I was travelling the world.

"We can't go anywhere, we won't be able to leave the U.K., the flights are grounded, boats are docked in ports. Trains and buses are still running, but you need a government key worker pass to use them."

"Well, that's just stupid. I am so bored, this is so boring. So, Mum, what can I do today?"

"You're making me cross, Bernice, I haven't got the answers to all of your questions, just get out from underneath my feet."

I knew that was a warning; on this occasion I chose to ignore it.

"I'm sooooo bored."

"Please stop whining in my ear, just go to your room and entertain yourself. I really have got to leave for work."

"You've got an empty brain."

I marched off in a huff to my bedroom, thinking maybe Google would have the answers I was searching for.

My bedroom.

Imagine a large room with wooden floorboards, a high ceiling and built-in wardrobes.

I am a collector of stuff, a hoarder; tin cans, yoghurt pots of all shapes and sizes, two-litre pop bottles. My collection also included newspapers, tin foil and flattened cardboard boxes. In my wardrobe it was incredibly full of all of these sorts of items; all labelled precisely and organised into plastic tubs on shelving, one tub next to another.

In the far corner of my room was a sixteen-cube Ikea kallax unit, with brightly coloured boxes, each box labelled like the wardrobe storage. This was a collection of all the 'other' bits I often discovered, whether that was from a skip or from beside the roads near to where I lived. An awesome collection of car hub caps, bike pedals and wheels. Then there was also chicken wire, bits of wood and old keys.

Everything was catalogued on a spreadsheet on my iPad.

I was an entrepreneur of waste. I made it my business to provide newspapers to schools in my area for those making papier mâché projects or yoghurt pot robots.

I was well known in my town, and my mum had no idea. Access was restricted into my bedroom, a huge sign reading 'Berni's Recycling Centre KEEP OUT' on the door. Only I had the keys to my room, always in a pocket. When Mum occasionally got a glimpse she called it the dump.

The door to my bedroom had ten padlock locks, all in a variety of sizes, which I had found over the years. When I spotted a new one, it was added to my door on returning home. After all, my work was important and I didn't need prying eyes, asking what I was up to.

Mum was often puzzled. The recycling bin never had any rubbish in it, and yet it had been like this for years, so she assumed I was being a good girl and doing my household chores, but there was something else going on; she just couldn't put her finger on it.

Mum had left for work, I knew she had by the slam of the front door, the noise rattling through the house like a reverberating shockwave. I knew that my mum was angry with me. I watched out of my window as Mum made the journey down the street to the bus stop. Tears formed in her eyes and slowly trickled down her face; she hated this life and it felt like she was stuck in a goldfish bowl, swimming around and around and every now and then bumping up against the glass.

Mum was sad, annoyed at herself for losing her temper, slamming the door on her way out. Out of her handbag came a mobile device, the number dialled, a ringtone was heard and then the answerphone message kicked in: "Hi, this is Berni, or Bernice if you're Mum! I am unable to pick up my phone right now, because I am off on a world adventure. Please leave me a message and I might get back to you in the future."

"Bernice, Bernice, it's Mum, erm, I am sorry, love, for getting so annoyed with you. On my way home from work later on I'll see if I can pick up your favourite chocolate bar."

I heard the phone ring and ring off. I didn't answer and the answerphone message was ignored.

I plugged in my printer and sat down at my desk,

switching the Apple iPad on. The Google search bar loaded up, and I typed in 'how to travel the world from your bedroom'.

"50 Travel-Themed Home Décor Accessories to Affirm Your..."

"156 Best Travel-Themed Bedroom images..."

This wasn't what I'd had in mind at all, so next I typed in 'famous landmarks around the world'.

"London – Big Ben Clock tower..."

"Egypt – Pyramids – Ancient masonry structures built as tombs for pharaohs..."

"China – The Great Wall of China – A historical place in Beijing – One of the Seven Wonders of the World..."

Wow, all of these amazing landmarks, I can recreate them from my recycling collection. The printer whirred into life as it began to print out the images that I had selected: Big Ben, Egyptian Pyramids and The Great Wall of China. With the images printed and now laid out in front of me, I started to write notes on each picture with what materials to construct them.

Big Ben: a tall, vertical, rectangular-shaped building, linked to a horizontal rectangle building (called Westminster) in eight sections, with a large clock on the tower with a numbered dial and hands.

- Rectangular boxes (cereal sort)
- Paints, brushes, scissors, superglue
- Large white plastic plate
- Bike parts and yoghurt pots.

Egyptian Pyramids: four large triangles, brick detail, doorway and hieroglyphs.

- Four large triangles of wood
- Four long slats of wood to make pyramid frame, smaller pieces to add across horizontally
- Nails, hammer, jigsaw.

I was a highly skilled and self-taught maker of stuff; I had watched hundreds of YouTube tutorials.

The Great Wall of China: a large winding walkway, with walls on either side, castle turrets and forts, green bushes, plants and trees.

- Long lengths of wood (frame making) flatter pieces for walkways
- Plyboard cut out into wall pieces and for turrets
- Jigsaw, nails
- Soil, cement
- Grey spray paint

I would incorporate my long garden into this construction, it had large bushes, trees and greenery; the wall would fit perfectly into the space.

I started with Big Ben. I could construct this in my bedroom. It would be easy, assembling the parts, everything within easy reach from my wardrobes. Following my own plan, I began to place all the parts together, one piece on top of another, using the super strong glue to attach the black metal strips to make the hands on the clock. Then out came the paints and paintbrushes for all the final delicate details. The finished Big Ben towered above me. My bedroom had a high ceiling and my model nearly reached it. Looking up at the creation, I was mesmerised by its grandeur and I could understand why it was an iconic landmark.

For my next model it was time to move outside, which meant moving a lot of my bedroom outside: wood, power tools, work bench.

In the shed, I found the other things that were needed: spade, cement and the spirt level. I opened the patio door and found the extension lead, taking string and wooden pegs, the area was mapped out for the Pyramid. The ground was quite soft because at the beginning of the year it had rained a lot. Using the spade, the first trench was made. A total of four trenches were needed for the four wooden struts to sit into, which would form part of the strong frame to attach the large triangles needed for each side.

The outdoor tap was near to the kitchen and easily accessible for the three parts water to two large scoops of quick dry extra strong cement. I used a large stick to mix the sloppy mixture. Then, carefully carrying the bucket back to the Pyramid site, I tipped some of the cement into the first hole, then placed the long large thick wooden strut. To support this, whilst trying alone to construct the rest, I had made props to sit on either side, so that the strut would dry into the correct position. I quickly repeated the same method for the other three struts and, to make sure the point at the top was sitting in the right position, I had to climb up the stepladder to the top step.

Whilst the struts were drying, I took myself off to the loo and made some lunch.

A doorway had to be cut into one of the triangles, and then the nailing began. On went the horizontal strips, one after another. These were not as thick as the struts and were being used to brace the underneath of the structure. After this job was completed, the outer four large side panels could be nailed onto the frame. These were marine plyboard sheets, waterproof and rescued from a skip down the road.

I stood back in awe of this amazing structure before me. It had taken me all of my morning to form the outside, it took the Egyptians thousands of years. If I could have built mine of stone, I would have dedicated my life to the building of these magnificent monuments. I still had the finishing touches to do, the hieroglyphic doorway and the outer spray-painted brick detailing.

My phone rang. It was mum. I didn't pick up.

"Hi, Bernice, it's Mum. I will be catching the 6pm bus home, please put the tea on later, love, it's been a really long, hard day, and I will be too tired to cook when I get in."

I didn't want to speak to Mum. I was imagining what it would have been like to be an Egyptian princess, to live near and sail on the Nile, to be pampered day and night. A romantic view about how life might have been thousands of years ago.

I had a great imagination for a thirteen-year-old girl.

Finally, the last construction, saving the best for last, the Seventh Wonder of the World, a construction so large it could be seen from space. The Great Wall of China in my garden, a doorway to Beijing's mountain ranges. All of this filled me with great excitement. Amazing ideas pinged and bounced around inside my head as I began my third and final model.

I mapped out the ground between the shrubs and trees. The plan was to build a raised walkway initially. I calculated that thirty-two holes in the ground were needed, evenly spaced, and into these holes would go vertical struts, four in each section. In total, there would be eight sections. Each section would be made into large square-like boxes, and across each box would be slats (like the sort you find underneath a mattress, on a wooden bed frame). Then on top of this, larger pieces of flat wooden sheets would be nailed down to form the flooring.

I gathered all the tools I needed to start working:

- Thirty-two wooden struts each measuring 182.88cm (6ft)
- Thirty-two flat wooden sides (four for each box)
- Ninety-six flat wooden strips (twelve for each box)
- Cement mixed in the bucket, work bench, power tools
- Nails.

I took the spade and dug hole one of thirty-two, and on until all the holes had been created. Quick dry cement into every hole, one, two, three, four struts (fence posts) into each hole to form a square, one of eight completed, seven more to go.

Four side panels added to each square box, twelve slats across each top and the flat panel for flooring.

Along the sides, boarding cut out into turret shapes placed at different heights and at two points along the stretch for the fort-like buildings.

Along the walkway, the piles of discarded stones from around the garden and remaining cement to fix these to the wood. Once dried, grey spray paint to make it look like grey cobbled stones, a proper winding footpath.

With remaining wood, steps were created up to the walkway, then lengths of wood cut from the struts to make everything level. Next the brick detail on the inside and outside of the walls, with brushes and spray paints I had discovered in the garage.

As I stepped onto my creation, I arrived at the seventh wonder. Standing in my shorts and vest, I suddenly felt really chilly. It was raining, light drizzle fell against my face, the wind whipped my hair around. Instead of standing still, I started to explore the vast pathway in front of me. I was amazed at the awesome views of the mountains, some snow-capped. This was amazing! I peered over the wall edges, fascinated by the sounds of the birds in the trees, so much to take in and see.

The day had passed slowly, immersed in my work; I hadn't realised what the time was.

Mum had arrived home from her long shift at

work, hot and bothered after sitting on an airless bus, unlocking the front door. Needing a wee, she made her way up the stairs. To get to the bathroom, she had to pass my bedroom. The door was open; no sight of me, but a whole lot of mess, stuff all over the place. It looked like someone had burgled my room! Then Mum spotted the very large model of 'Big Ben' standing in the middle of the room.

Making her way downstairs, she saw more scattered stuff. Feeling worried, she called out, "Bernice, Bernice, where are you?" No answer. Mum crept to the patio door in the dining room. The first thing she saw was this huge Pyramid-like construction. She didn't know what to think as she walked her way around it. Still no sign of me, she started to feel anxious and panicked, then to her right she spotted something else. It was a huge construction. Mum climbed the wooden steps and that's when she saw me, so she called out, "Bernice, WHAT ON EARTH IS ALL OF THIS BLOODY MESS DOING IN MY GARDEN?!"

I was exploring The Great Wall. What was that noise? It sounded like someone shouting, but there was no one else with me.

"Bernice!"

Mum made her way onto the wall and grabbed my arm.

"Arrrrrrrghhhhh, what is happening?!"

I was being dragged backwards.

"Bernice, stop screaming, the neighbours will call the police, you stupid girl!"

I was hysterical by this point; I knew this voice well, it was Mum's. "Mum, you're hurting me, let go!"

Mum let go, her face beetroot red with rage. "So what is all of this, what have you done to my beautiful garden?"

"Mum, that is a pyramid from Egypt, and this is The Great Wall of China," Berni explained through her tears.

"Bernie, this is a mess, which you are now going to tidy up and then you're grounded for the rest of this week."

Years ago, before Mum had me, she had been a young student on her gap year, travelling to all seven wonders of the world. The last one had been The Great Wall of China. This is where she had met my dad.

"Mum, it isn't a mess, it's The Great Wall of China; look, come and see with me."

Mum wasn't sure but curiously she took my hand. I led her up the steps and, as both of our feet touched the walkway, we were transported together. Mum was back on this amazing landmark. It looked just like it had years ago. She felt the rain and the wind. Mum didn't know what to think; was this real or a dream? In the distance, we could both see another person. Who was it and why were they there. Holding each other's hands, we both stepped forward.

"Mum, it's a man, who is it?"

"Bernice, love, that's your dad."

We both walked forward, and then the three of us embraced each other in a hug.

★★★

Charlotte Ryan, aged 40, is a dyslexic mother of two. She runs her own business in childcare. She is also a social entrepreneur, waste reduction consultant, community support, event planner and organiser. She is the founder of WasteNot Leicestershire Reduce, Re-use Recycle: a Facebook group with over 9,000 members, and of The Leicestershire Community Cupboard, a self-funded project that has supported hundreds of people across Leicestershire with material support in the last two and a half years. From clothing to household items, donated and redistributed by Charlotte with volunteers.

★★★

I dedicate my story to my dad, who nears the end of his amazing life, for giving me a life full of opportunities, love, courage and understanding.

STILL HERE

Paula Robbins

Why is it that you are always fighting? I don't mean physically, but I do mean mentally and emotionally. You do it so often you wonder if there is a finish line and, if there is, where the hell is it?

I've always been a fighter by nature, I guess. It seemed to be the only way to get anywhere. I fought my family, I literally fought for a career, then I fought my mind. I'll let you decide which was the hardest.

It took me years and years to realise that fighting everyone and everything was doing nothing more than ramping my blood pressure up. Let me see if I can explain.

I guess it started before I left home but that is not a story for now. It started when I left home and joined the Army, in less than ideal circumstances, but you work with what you've got. It continued into basic training when you have thirty women in your platoon all shouting 'look at me'. Can I just say oh my God regarding the gossip! I'd never known anything quite like it. You fight to achieve, to grow up, to grow, to win, to be the best you can be. If you manage to navigate that rocky road that has to be a win, right? Ah but then, then comes trade training, which is a whole different ball game. So now you are fighting men and women for your 'look at me' moments.

If you are lucky enough, you navigate through that quagmire of personalities and emerge qualified and victorious. So, you've won and no longer need to fight, right? Wrong! Because next you hit your attachment with already established groups and cliques. Oh boy was that an eye opener! So, then you fight to establish yourself and show that you can actually do the job. Sounds easy, huh? Maybe it was just me, because easy is not the word I would use. Did I enjoy the challenge? Sure did. Did I enjoy being a part of a special group of people? Certainly. Did I enjoy hiding who I was and burying the essence of me? Hell no!

So, I fought that too.

Okay, so after five years, you come to the stunning realisation that you really don't want to do this any more and need to leave. Easier said than done! So, you work A YEAR of notice and leave. Completely unprepared for life outside of the micro world you've been living in. Oh my hell! This was trickier than anything I'd managed before; people were so complicated! Instead of going home, you end up in a very large city surrounded by exceptionally busy strangers with opaque intentions. You learn very quickly that more fighting is needed, on a level you haven't before experienced. You fight to live, to eat, to work. You fight your past and your horrors. But you slowly win your fight. Trouble is, you win by conforming, not by being unique. By being you.

So, I moved into a job and found that my particular experiences and skills were brilliant at it, made for it in a way. However, I started to die inside again, a slow drip, then a torrent. It was soul destroying.

Disastrous relationships aside, in which I was still fighting, and a job that was eating me alive. Not better off after all. After seven soul destroying years, I move again.

I'm still fighting.

New county, new city, new job, new partner. What could go wrong? Everything, it seems. Why? Because now I wasn't fighting to be noticed or to be promoted. I wasn't fighting a good cause or the side of democracy. Oh no, I was fighting me. I was fighting my past, my thoughts, my feelings. It was invisible but tangible. It was silent but shouting at the same time. This time, I no longer fought, I sank.

I plodded along, going through the motions of life. Not completely down and out, but not far from it. Treading water, so to speak. The thoughts I had and words I needed to speak didn't come as easily any more. Did I need a life raft? Kind words? Time? It seems I needed only one of those, possibly not the one you thought.

I needed time. But I needed it with someone that would reignite the fight. That would relight the stubborn contrariness that is me. To make me fight, not the world, but myself.

Be careful what you wish for!

This fight. These thoughts, my mind. Lost for so very long, sparked. Then it rumbled and almost became indignant that someone dared to wake it up. Over a short period of time it seems as though my thoughts and voice became one. And they had a lot to say!

So where does that leave me today?

More focused? Hmm, not particularly. More centred? Definitely. More at peace? God yes.

At this point I can say I'm still here, still loving and being loved. Still working through my thoughts and dreams. Still being snarky, sarcastic and mouthy.

So yeah, here I am today, still fighting.

And you know what? That is not a bad thing.

★★★

Paula Robbins is originally from Cambridge but now resides in Leicestershire with her wife of three years Louise and their crazy cat. Paula currently works in Social Care but is retraining as a proofreader. Paula loves to read fantasy/alternative fiction and is a bit of a history buff.

DREAM CONNECTION

Ruby Perry

Sometimes not having a voice results in unkind comments, hair pulling, shoving. It sounds a lot like bullying, but it's not to me. I deserve it — I choose to be quiet, and if I try to speak the words get caught in my throat and I sit there opening and closing my mouth. I used to get asked if I was related to the fish family.

Sometimes having a voice results in unkind comments, because it can be too loud and irritating. That used to be me. But that's what I am weary of now. If I am too loud, I will be asked questions I don't want to be asked, and that's not a nice feeling. I'll be asked where my mum is and I will have to explain that she died when I lived in Yorkshire, so then I moved in with Dad who lived all the way in Glasgow. It's not wrong to speak, unless you're me, because it was me speaking that made me lose friends and family. The words I said were never going to be taken back; I was a bully. When Mum died, I went into self-destruct and realised what I did made other people unhappy. I decided to not say anything after that, and since then it's hard for even the smallest words to be said, even though they're kind.

I remember the day I was told that Mum had died. I was sitting in a room all alone waiting for her to return home from work. Beside me I had a tray of delicious homemade pastries and a warm mug of coffee. I had used Mum's favourite teapot and mug set and laid fresh strawberries and raspberries in a heart shape on a silver plate. We had had an argument in the morning and as I left for school I shouted, "I hate you!" and slammed the door. Mum usually went shopping on a Thursday, so I expected her to be later, but as I waited up it began to grow dark and hours flew by; eight to nine, nine to ten, ten to eleven. Then finally there was a knock. I sleepily jumped up – tipping over the cold tea, it was like a shock against my bare foot. I hunted for the key and headed to the door. The figure outside wasn't my mum's. I stopped in my tracks as I had been told to never answer the door to strangers. As I was turning to walk back into my room, the doorbell rang. It echoed in my ears and filled the whole house with music. "It's the police," a voice boomed as it rang out into the empty darkness. I cautiously opened the door and then the news was told…

I moved up to my dad's house two days later. However hard he tried, it still felt lonely. Within a few weeks of living there, I discovered a cherry blossom tree that bloomed all spring and summer long. I would sit under there and lose myself in a book or scroll through the endless pictures of me on my mum's Instagram; I seemed so happy.

The tree gave me inspiration and it encouraged my tendency to help others. Since being a bully, I had changed and my heart was softer and my soul was brighter; it didn't mean they weren't fragile though. I set up a page on Instagram called 'agony.aUnt33'. Although I was under-age, my mum allowed me to have an account under her supervision. The new page was used to help young girls and boys like me who were searching for their voices. I wrote my first post the minute I opened the account.

> ⋆Hi, this is a page for children aged 10+ who have lost their voice. Or are searching for it. Sometimes when bad things happen or you do bad things, you punish yourself – I did it by stopping myself from talking. As a 12-year-old myself I did some things, things that I regret.
>
> *And yes, you can't take them back, but you can change what you do,* what you say. If you feel the slightest bit upset, feel free to dm me. ⋆

Days passed and I amused myself by reading and going to the local park. I was eager to see how many comments I had got and so logged onto Instagram the next week. FIFTY-TWO NOTIFICATIONS! Oh wow, I was so shocked, I had to take a seat. I had over 860 followers already and forty-nine direct messages.

SMILEYBecca 12
★I have been like that for ages! Keep posting. I will look daily. ★

MaXNeLSoN 10_08
★Thanks, you are so brave to do this★

JESS.SlnGsss.9
★*Cool*★

11.alisoN_ANDREWS
★*I am always alone, I have lost my voice, my only ever friend – she moved-house. I need someone…*★

The last one stood out to me. My best friend from Yorkshire was called Alison Anderson and the name had such a likeness that it touched me. It would break my heart to ever think she could feel like that. So, I replied:

agony.aUnt33
★*So sorry to hear you feel this way. I can relate. DM me! I'll try you*★

I went onto my direct messages and felt a bit overwhelmed. Usually when I get like that, I have a panic attack, so I tried the method that my therapist taught me:

Breath in
Hold
Out
In
Hold
Out
Repeat

I scrolled down my followers page until I reached her name. With a deep breath I typed her a message. I wasn't sure what to put, so I just went on my own experiences and sent her it. she replied straight away.

Days flew by, and we texted regularly. It went from winter to spring and spring to summer.

Me: Hi Alison, is it? I read your message, sorry.
Alison: Thanks, what's your name? So I know what to call you.
Me: I did say I was staying anonymous, but it won't hurt to tell you. Lottie Bakewell. Do you have a nickname?
Alison: Yep, Ali.
Me: OK Ali, are you bullied?
Ali: Yep.
Me: Do you live here?
Ali: Where?
Me: Glasgow.
Ali: Oh, yeah!
Me: So, do you go to my school?

Ali: Yep.
Me: There are bullies at Cherry High?
Ali: Uh huh.
Me: OK. Where do you stay in the playground? I will look out for you?
Ali: By the gate. Got to go, bye.

We hadn't texted much after that; it made me wonder what she was like. I looked out for her in the playground but didn't often see her. Every day I stood at the gates and waited. I saw a strange man staring at me yesterday, he stood outside of the school. As soon as I made eye contact with him, he left. He may have spotted something over my shoulder, but I looked back and the playground was empty, the last few children running indoors before the second bell went.

His face was in the centre of my mind all day, I couldn't get rid of it.

When I got home, I texted dad to tell him I had arrived home safely. Then I found Ali's account and messaged her.

Me: Did you see that man today?
Ali: YES! He was tall, with dark brown hair. He didn't see me, hbu?
Me: He saw me, and then ran off. He looked very old – at least 50 – lol. ☺
Ali: Oh. Cool.
Me: I am bored. Want to go park?

Me: Ali?
Ali: Which one?
Me: BY THE CHERRY TREE.
Ali: Let me see…

Ali: SOS taking cat to the vets… Uh.
Me: OK text you later.

I don't know why I offered to meet her, I was bored, and she was usually alone.

I always feel embarrassed when I go to the park because there are loads of groups of kids but I am alone. Usually I just climb up the biggest tree and sit, sucking on a toffee and gazing out on the rooftops from the nearby village, but today I sat on the swing and let my feet glide through the air as they were elevated by the force.

When I put my feet on the uneven ground, I stumbled as the swing still rocked forwards and backwards. My toffees fell out of my pocket as I steadied myself and got back on the seat with a jump. A man walked over and handed them to me. He had a very familiar appearance and I knew I had seen it before. But where? He smiled at me and his golden tooth shone in the light, his breath smelt of garlic and he had hairy warts.

Alison hadn't messaged me for ages, I would sit and stare at her account; her profile photo portrayed a beautiful girl with short red hair. Sometimes I would scroll through her photos. It struck me that she never uploaded photos of herself, just quotes!

I tried messaging her again.

Me: Hey Ali.
Ali: Hi ☺
Me: My dad gave me some money do u want to go shopping?
Ali: OK where shall I meet you?
Me: Primark? It is my favourite store.
Ali: Yeppity doo.
Me: lol, see you in 10.

Eleven minutes later, I arrived at Primark. It was useful having a shopping centre that was only a short bus ride away. I stood patiently at the entrance waiting for Alison to turn up. A man bumped into me because his eyes were glued to his phone. He looked up and smiled at me apologetically. Another golden tooth; *They must be in fashion*, I thought… but the man did seem familiar. He put his phone in his pocket and turned around, just as I got a message from Alison.

Ali: ARGHHH can't make it, Mum taking me 2 theme park 4 a treat! Happy but sad
Me: Uh, have fun… send me a pic?
Ali: Can't, my camera isn't working.

ODD.

Never mind, I told myself. I can still have fun. I bought myself some ripped jeans, a checked t-shirt, an Adidas sweater and a pleated skirt. And thankfully I arranged a place to meet Ali the next day. That night I chose my outfit to wear to the cafe – a lilac sweatshirt with girl power on it, some comfy Nike leggings and a pair of white Converse. Next to my bed was a photo of Mum and me in matching make-up hugging each other. I kissed the cold glass before making myself comfy. The last few days had been busy and the minute I touched the pillow I was asleep.

Mum reached out to me and pulled me close. I moved but there was nothing on me but light. I attempted to hug Mum, but my arms reached right through her. "Where am I?" I shouted (the first sentence I had properly said since she had died). "Am I in heaven?" I screamed, eager for an answer. "No, my dear, you are dreaming, of course," Mum replied.

"I did bad things" I cried.

"And I forgive you."

"I can't take them back."

"You have made up for it."

"Why am I here?"

"Because I need to say something," Mum said.

"What?"

"Lottie, you are here for a short time – you have five minutes left and this is important."

"Okay, what?"

"Uh..."

"Mum?" I shouted.

"Okay, just don't believe everything that's behind or on a screen."

"Why?"

"Your time is up; I say no more," she said and walked off.

"Mum?" I whispered.

"MUM?" I screamed. "I love you."

As she walked into the foggy distance, she said, "I love you too."

I woke up in a bundle of sheets, sweat sticking to the mattress. I checked the time: 7:42. It made me laugh that such a short dream took up a whole night's sleep. What did Mum mean, 'Don't always believe what's behind a screen?'

Then it clicked: Alison.

Who was she, or he? How did I know she was my age? Why hadn't I seen her at school? Why did she always cancel when we arranged to meet up? It was like a jigsaw with missing pieces.

Suddenly I felt sick to my stomach. We were meeting that day. I had to cancel.

Me: Can't come. Am ill, soz.

It was very blunt, very brisk, but I was scared. It was that same feeling I had the night Mum died. That shaken up sensation.

I just went back to bed all day. I dwelled on it for hours and it exhausted my brain until I eventually fell asleep. The next day the post came through the letterbox. Dad was at work again, so I collected it and sat on the sofa to read it. A certain page caught my eye:

11.alisoN_ANDREWS
do not believe HIM

That's right, HIM! 50 year old man has forged a young girl's account on Instagram and has messaged vulnerable people, getting information on where they live and go. The man is currently on the run and the police have no details on his appearance. GIRLS in Glasgow who have been tricked by this man, can you please report to the police if you have seen a man in his 50s numerous times after telling "ALISON" where you were. DO NOT WORRY – INVESTIGATION IS IN PROGRESS!

OMG, Mum was right. I grabbed my phone from the coffee table and googled ALISON ANDREWS MALE. I clicked on images and loads of pictures appeared – all of different men that I had never seen before, except one.

Hairy warts. Check.

Gold tooth. Check.

Socks with sandals. Check. Underneath the photo was a link:

www.AliAndrews.lnstagram.com ALI, then I remembered where I saw him.

School – I told Alice about Cherry High
Park – I told Alice to meet me there
Shops – We were going to buy stuff.

A few days later

I told the police everything – and Dad promised to spend more time with me. That man – Ali – had escaped prison in Lancashire where he was sentenced for murder. So, I saved people's lives. No, Mum did.

He was caught trying to smuggle a young girl out to sea. She returned safely home, because of Mum.

He is back in prison, because of Mum.

Mum forgave me for what I did, and I could never be more grateful.

★★★

Ruby Perry is eleven years old and lives in Leicestershire. She discovered her love of reading and writing at an early age. She loves all books but especially historical fiction. Her dream is to become an author. She also enjoys dancing and being with her friends and family. If you'd like to get in touch then you can do so via Fuzzy Flamingo: contact@fuzzyflamingo.co.uk

BOXED IN

Jen Parker

Florrie stared at the feathers falling through her fingers with tears streaming down her face, feeling nothing short of devastated. She could feel the wings crumbling, the feelings of elation crumbling with them. Could it be over as suddenly as that?

★

It was a lonely existence under the watchful eye of an overbearing father and no friends or family to rescue her. Florrie was confined to her room for most of the day every day. She was only allowed out to eat her meals with her father at the dining table, where he'd test her general knowledge and maths skills, and quiz her on what she'd learnt from her tutor that day.

"If you want to go far in life, you need to learn about how the world works," he'd say. But Florrie would think to herself *Surely I need to go out into the world to learn how it works.* But she wouldn't dare to say it out loud. She'd attempted to talk to her father about it once, which had resulted in the worst beating he'd ever given her with his belt. She was soon cowed into silence and didn't dare to say anything else that wasn't a direct answer to his questions.

Florrie's mother had walked out on the family when she was only a few months old. It was never explained to her what had happened, only that she'd left and that she wasn't to be talked about under any circumstances. Her father had raised her on his own, and it was just the two of them in their third-floor two-storey apartment. Florrie knew they were wealthy, but didn't know what her father did for a living. He'd leave early in the morning after her tutor had arrived for the day and arrive home in time for their evening meal together.

She'd tried to talk to her tutor about her situation only once. The colour had drained from Carla's face and she'd looked visibly frightened. "I mustn't comment on any family's lives, each parent has the right to parent in their own way," she said. Florrie had tried to protest and ask more questions, but she was shut down so quickly she hadn't attempted another probe.

She felt isolated, cut off from the outside world. She wasn't even allowed to watch television. She occasionally watched her neighbour's television through her binoculars from her bedroom window. They had a very young child and often had the subtitles on to save the risk of waking her, so Florrie was able to watch the odd programme. But it wasn't easy to do and wasn't exactly light relief.

Carla was packing up her bag at the end of the school day when she looked over her shoulder at the door. Florrie's father was due back at any moment. In hushed tones, she spoke to Florrie as she drew a small box out of her bag.

"This may help you with your loneliness," she said conspiratorially.

"What is it?" asked Florrie, as she gazed in wonder at the small, engraved wooden box. The carvings of feathers and birds were exquisite. The gleam of the polished wood caught the light from the spotlights making it seem almost iridescent. It was like no wood she'd seen before.

"Whenever you're feeling low, hold it close and think of what you'd like to change. Then open it and see what happens. It only serves those truly in need. Now run and hide it in your bedroom. And under no circumstances let anybody else see it."

When Florrie returned to the study, Carla had packed her remaining belongings and was just closing the final clasp of her bag when they heard her father's key in the door. They looked at each other and, for the first time, a look passed between them that felt electric. It was the first connection with a person that Florrie had ever felt and she never wanted it to end; she could almost feel a buzz of electricity flowing through her. But the entrance of her father interrupted their gaze and the connection broke in an instant.

That night, Florrie gazed at the box in her hands. It was slightly larger than her hands, but light enough to hold in one. The feeling of emptiness, of being alone, of not having anyone but her own thoughts for company almost consumed her. But then her thoughts returned to the eye contact she'd held with Carla. There was something different in that look, something that made her feel that maybe she wasn't alone. Did Carla care about her? She looked again at the box and a shimmer seemed to pass over the lid. It was as if it were glowing, although she couldn't see light coming from it anywhere. It was more like a feeling that it could glow. She thought again about her loneliness, then of Carla, and held the box tightly, drawing it into her chest.

Was it trembling? She drew the box back out to look at it again but the trembling stopped. Was it her? Was she trembling? She held it tight and the trembling started again almost immediately. And could it be warm? It certainly felt like it was emanating a warmth that was flowing through her. She pulled the box away from her and looked at it closely. The trembling and the warmth faded, but the surface of the lid shimmered once more. It couldn't just be the reflection of the lights, could it? There were too many colours in the shimmer to be from her white bedroom light. She took in a big breath, closed her eyes and held the box as tightly to her chest as she could.

The trembling grew and grew and became a shudder and a shake. The warmth grew and grew and passed through her in waves, feeling like it was warming her to her very core, her very soul. Just as she thought she might have to let it go because it was shuddering so hard, the shaking and the warmth stopped dead. She let out the breath she hadn't even realised she'd been holding. She opened her eyes, wondering if she'd see anything different, be anywhere different. But there were the same four walls she felt imprisoned within every single day, the same old bed that offered no respite from the loneliness, the same window that teased her with glimpses of an exciting world outside.

Nothing had changed.

Nothing.

She should have known. She didn't even know what she'd expected. It was just her. It was always just her.

She put the box down on the bed and sighed deeply. Something caught her eye. She glanced at the box and it snatched her attention fully. It was no longer just shimmering and the glow was more than just a feeling; it was sending out beams of light, which were now bouncing off her bedroom walls. She dived on it with worry that it might catch the attention of her father. With one sweep, she picked up the box and opened it in one smooth motion. The light faded and the box stilled in her hands. Sitting in the bottom of the box was a single white feather. It filled the length of the box, and was sparkling and beautiful.

As soon as Florrie picked up the feather, she felt a tingling running all through her body, which then focused on two points on her back. Then with a whoosh, two huge white wings sprouted from her shoulder blades and raised high above her head. She looked up in amazement, but felt a strange sense of calm, as if she had always known they could come.

Florrie walked to the window with her head held high, knowing exactly what she was meant to do. She opened the window wide, climbed onto the windowsill and, without hesitation, thrust herself into the evening sky. The sun was descending, casting a warm orange and red glow across the sky, and the air smelled clean and warm and inviting. She didn't even have to think about it, she instinctively knew how to flap her wings when she needed to rise, hold them to soar and glide and turn her body and her wings to direct herself.

She soared as high as she dared into the sky, feeling the warm air rush against her skin and flow through her hair. As she glided around her quiet neighbourhood, she looked at all the houses far below and felt a longing to see the people inhabiting them, to feel a connection. She flew lower and peeked in windows as she glided past, catching glimpses of the lives of others. Some were eating a late dinner, some were reading stories to children, others basked in the warm glow of televisions.

Florrie's attention was drawn to one house in particular. She circled the roof a couple of times before she risked a look in the windows. Diving down to the top window, she nearly fell from the sky with her shock.

There, standing in front of her, as if she knew when she'd come, was Carla. The bedroom window was flung open as Florrie composed herself and flapped gently to rise back up to be level with it. Carla's penetrating eyes were upon her, but they held so much warmth that she felt like she was holding the glowing box again. Tentatively, Florrie flew to the window and, with the help of Carla, climbed in.

Without a second thought, the first thing Florrie did was to fling her arms around Carla, who reciprocated with the first hug Florrie had ever received. Her heart felt as if it were growing, fit to burst with the happiness she felt. Carla beckoned her over to sit down on one of the chairs in the room and they had their first frank and honest talk in the whole time they'd known each other. It was such a relief to finally talk to someone about her father and the way she lived her life, and Carla listened intently and with great compassion.

Although she wasn't surprised or shocked to hear Florrie's tales, Carla was still greatly saddened to hear it from her. She reassured Florrie that they couldn't let it continue and that they'd get the help she needed. They put together a plan of action to involve the authorities and Florrie was to keep a diary every day about her experiences. She was also to hide secret cameras about the house and even on her person to gather evidence.

After what felt like hours of talking, Florrie and Carla finally said emotional goodbyes. Florrie took off through the window and, after exploring for a bit longer until the chill of the night started seeping into her bones, she went home to her bedroom window.

Almost as soon as she landed in her bedroom, she felt different. She looked around at the space enclosing her and felt that finally it wasn't going to be like this forever, there was a light at the end of the tunnel. And with that, she felt her wings tumbling down on themselves, the feathers from the top cascading down to the bottom until they had all disintegrated. She held her hands out to try and stop them, to try and catch them before they fell, but it was no use.

Florrie stared at the feathers falling through her fingers with tears streaming down her face, feeling nothing short of devastated. She could feel the wings crumbling, the feelings of elation crumbling with them. Could it be over as suddenly as that?

A lone feather drifted down in front of her and she watched as it fell in slow motion, swaying left and right as it descended. It fell into the open box on the bed in front of her and looked exactly like that first feather had when she'd opened the box. She drew the box to her and gently closed the lid.

Her first flight may have been over, but her freedom was just beginning.

★★★

Jen Parker is from Leicester, she's a mum of two girls and is in her thirties. This is her first work of fiction, although she's a published bestselling author of non-fiction. She's the owner of Fuzzy Flamingo providing editing, design and publishing services and putting this book together has been an absolute joy!

www.fuzzyflamingo.co.uk

LESSONS OF LIFE, LOVE AND FEAR

Laura Goodsell

It all began back in January, a month that brought freezing weather and a freezing absence in my heart. Little did I know that from that day when Simon left me and, as the months began to warm up and my heart thawed, things would get a lot hotter than I expected.

Simon and I had been together for three years. I thought they were happy years but I was so blinded by love. Coming home from work one evening, I found that he and all his belongings had gone. That was it, just like that it was all over.

I got on the phone to him straight away. At the time I believed him when he said he just needed space. So, you can imagine how hurt I was when I saw him a couple of weeks later with Mandy Richards in town. It was snowing heavily at this point and all I could think about was ramming a huge snowball in her face. I didn't, of course, I kept my dignity, walked home and cried myself to sleep. So, a crappy start to the new year. Well, things can only get better, as the saying goes.

At the beginning of March, I got called into my

manager's office. I knew what was coming, I'd been a lousy employee the past year, especially since Simon left me. Sitting in Mr Cohan's tiny office at the stationer's where I worked, I couldn't help but drift off into a daydream while I waited. I didn't hear when Mr Cohan came in, he made me jump when he boomed, 'Kate, I think we need to talk.' He sat down heavily in front of me. 'Things haven't been going too well lately,' he stated.

After a long discussion, it was clear I wasn't keeping my job. My poor timekeeping, organisational skills and head in the clouds were to blame. I feebly attempted to defend myself but it didn't work, I left his office feeling dreadful. You would think all this was enough, but no, life had more in store for me.

It took me a while to fully accept that I'd lost my job. I'd hoped to have some sympathy from my mum, but no, all I got was, 'You idiot, I've been telling you for weeks this would happen.' I hated it so much, losing Simon and my job so close together. I just burst with anger at my mum. I knew I shouldn't have, but I couldn't help it. My mum and I are so very alike and stubborn, neither of us would apologise. It's regretful now because she's my mum and I love her. I realised I only shouted at her because we were so close. They always say you take it out on the ones you love most. So, I moved out the next day and crashed on my mate's sofa. I didn't want to stay long as she had a new baby and her own family to look after. The following morning, I dragged myself down to the local council office and signed up to the housing list.

A few days later, I was fortunate enough to get a small ground floor flat. It wasn't much, just a bedroom, living room and bathroom, but it did have a door out to a small courtyard area at the back. I felt things were looking up and the heartache of Simon was abating, although the argument with Mum still sat heavy with me.

I spent the next few weeks wandering around the charity shops in town, picking up bits for my new flat. I couldn't afford much as I had no job. I certainly couldn't afford to go into the city. I did manage to pick up a few nice bits and pieces, and a couple of friends also donated some bits as well. Towards the end of April, still with no job, the bills were mounting up, but the worst thing about it all was being lonely. I don't have a big family or a huge number of friends, so this was a really difficult time for me. What I needed was my mum.

At the beginning of May, the job hunt began with a fresh attitude, new month and all that. Although there wasn't a lot of choice, I did get a couple of interviews. One was at a new copy place in town; just a day to day assistant job, nothing glamorous, the same industry as my old job, so I felt more confident and uplifted. I tried not to get my hopes up as the pay was terrible, but went along and surprisingly got it.

On my first day I couldn't help thinking about Simon; this was something I would have shared with him. My thoughts of Simon didn't last as long these days, but a movie poster or little cafe would trigger a memory. So many memories but that's it, isn't it? They are just memories. I had to keep reminding myself that the future holds many more for me, good, bad and in-between.

My first day was pretty good. I met some lovely customers and all the employees were really friendly; one in particular caught my eye, his name was Christian and he had the most wonderful smile. Anyway, I was shattered by the time I got home, so had a long hot soak in the bath with a mountain of bubbles. I felt happy for what seemed like the first time in years. Unfortunately, these things don't last.

A few weeks into my new job and it was boring as hell. I had a job, at least, and life seemed to be picking up a bit. My birthday came around at the end of June. A day that I was dreading. With not having a boyfriend and arguing with my mum, I decided not to do a lot. The day started off normally enough; it was a Friday, so I was looking forward to the weekend. I got ready for work, ate breakfast and walked to work on my own. A couple of friends texted me happy birthday, and the guys at work clubbed together to get me a card and cake, plus I got to see Christian, an added bonus.

At 5:30pm I was getting ready to leave work when my mum called my mobile out of the blue; my heart skipped a beat when I saw her name. I have to admit, I'd been keeping an eye on my phone all day. I had very nearly caved and called her a few times, so I was thrilled when the phone rang.

She just said, 'Hi, love, happy birthday.' She sounded so sad. That was it, my emotions took over, tears trickled down my cheeks.

Just hearing her voice, I blurted out, 'Oh, Mum, I'm so sorry I've been such an idiot lately.' I completely caved in. She chuckled and sighed.

I asked, 'Can I come round?'

She responded, 'Of course you can, this is your home.'

After a few minutes, I put the phone down and went straight round Mum's. We both cried and talked for what felt like days.

I slept on Mum's sofa that night. I didn't feel like celebrating my birthday, so many mixed emotions, so Mum cooked spaghetti bolognese, my favourite, with garlic bread for tea to celebrate instead.

By the time I got back to my flat the next day, I felt physically and emotionally drained, but oh so happy, my heart lifted. I spent the Sunday in my PJs and relaxed all day. I felt so much better for it, I even ended up getting up on Monday morning in a reasonably good mood.

I saw Mum a few more times. Our relationship seemed to be improving. However, I stayed in my own flat. I felt I needed my own space now, I couldn't rely on my mum so much. We still saw each other a lot and, when we met up, we had so many exciting things to talk about and share.

July ended up being one of the hottest months on record. It was a pleasant time. I saw Mum more, things were good, I had my little job and I got to spend more time with Christian. We'd been getting on well at work and began socialising together. Often, we went to the pub and sat in the beer garden having a quiet drink. We just clicked, it felt good. What happened next did not, though, oh it didn't feel good at all.

Everything came to a standstill on the 7th August.

It was a normal Saturday. I was at home with Christian, planning on watching a DVD with a Chinese that evening. Around 7pm, we were deciding which film to watch. I was standing leaning against the radiator under the window, when after a few seconds it started to feel very warm.

I couldn't help thinking what a lovely warm breeze was wafting up the back of my t-shirt, but the breeze got hotter and hotter. Suddenly an image jumped into my mind and then it dawned on me what was happening. I looked over my shoulder and saw a flame, I was on fire! Panicked, I jumped forward, holding the shirt from my back. I wasn't really thinking straight, I knew I was on fire, but my mind was telling me not to be so stupid, things like that don't really happen. Luckily I didn't listen to my head, I listened to the heat and flame I could see over my shoulder.

Christian started shouting, 'Take your shirt off!'

I was shouting back, 'I can't! I can't!'

I froze. I remember Christian grabbing me and trying to rip the shirt at the neck, but as he pulled it towards him to rip it, the flames licked my back, and it burned too much, so I pulled away from him. I knew I had to get my shirt off, but I couldn't, I just couldn't do it, the fear had gripped me, so many thoughts rushing through my head all in a split second. I didn't want to set the flat on fire and remembered seeing in movies people on fire rolling in the snow, so I ran outside. No snow, obviously, just grass, it was August after all. I'd never felt panic like it before, I was terrified. I felt like I was going to die. The burning heat on my back was getting worse, I couldn't get my shirt off. I knew it was all psychological, my head was saying if I pull my shirt up over my head and it gets stuck, my head could catch fire. I just couldn't persuade my hands to do it.

I ran outside and hit the ground on my knees in total blind panic. Christian ran up to me and grabbed the bottom of the shirt, pulled it straight over my head as fast and hard as he could, and threw it on the grass. I was flooded with relief.

I sat down on the doorstep, feeling calmer but hazy; it was all over. A few minutes later, Christian followed me back inside. I could see him but didn't really notice him. He wanted me to put cold water on my back, but because I couldn't feel any pain, I told him I was fine, not to worry about me, I'd be fine. In the bathroom, I perched on the edge of the bath. I didn't care that I wasn't wearing a top, all sensation seemed to leave my body. Christian handed me the shower head and I held cold water on my back for a while. By this time the shock had kicked in and I couldn't stop shaking, even though I wasn't cold.

I reluctantly agreed to go to the hospital, as the burning was unbearable when I stopped the water. I eased on an old cotton shirt and joggers, and off we went. I looked a complete mess, my hair all wet and singed – actually very singed. My mum had to cut about four inches off just to get it level again. Luckily, she used to be a hairdresser when I was a kid.

The hospital staff were amazing. They gave me some painkillers and covered my back in this awesome cream, which instantly eased the pain. I was then wrapped in bandages and looked like an Egyptian mummy for the next two weeks. I was told I had suffered 4% first and second degree burns to my back. Ouch!

It was possibly the single scariest experience of my life. It's funny to look back on now, the thoughts that run through your head when you are faced with this kind of situation. I couldn't believe I thought it would actually snow in August, but I did at the time.

I had the next two weeks off work as I had three hospital appointments to change the bandaging and needed to rest. It was, strangely, a lovely time, as my mum and Christian both came round a lot to see me and check I was okay. It gave them a chance to finally meet and they got on really well. I went back to work afterwards and life settled down into a routine. That may have seemed boring to some, but I loved it.

So that's my story, it hasn't been a great year, but it has taught me a huge amount about myself and how strong I really am. Plus a few more important things along the way. I have learnt that life is very unpredictable and not to worry about things so much, to loosen control; trying to control everything causes more stress and anxiety. Money isn't everything but it does help pay the bills; I'm so thankful I have a job. I have also learnt to appreciate my life, even if it does veer off course occasionally and, most importantly, I have learnt to love and be thankful for – no matter what – my family and friends unconditionally, to tell them often, spend time with them and hold them close.

Because you never know what life may have in store for you.

★★★

Laura originates from Norfolk, but now lives in the East Midlands with her partner and their two boys, while running an award-winning small business, helping other business owners confidently grow online, by hosting WordPress and Canva workshops and courses, along with offering web design and social media services. Laura has also designed a collection of business planners available through Amazon:

www.anchoronline.co.uk

REFLECTIONS

Kate Carter

"Why do I even bother?" I looked at myself in the mirror, skin so pale that I looked ghostly.

Red marred my eyes from lack of sleep and, yep, was that another crease? Since losing my mum earlier in the year, I felt like I was scraping my way through every day. Suddenly I felt very old. I ached all over, my lower back was constantly giving me grief, but more than that. It was this feeling of being trapped by life. I mean, don't get me wrong, I loved my family. I had two kids and a husband who loved me and would do anything for me. Today was a great example. He'd said he was taking them to see his mum to give me some 'me' time. How lucky was I?! And yet I still woke up most mornings thinking, *Is this it, is this what life is about, just going through the motions?* I was such a selfish person. Why couldn't I just get over this already!

I was thirty-eight and it's like I'd suddenly woken up and thought, *What, I'm thirty-eight, where did my twenties go? What have I actually done with my life?* Every morning, I would wake with this emptiness inside, like I was missing something big. A pang of guilt hit me square in the stomach. I shouldn't be feeling this way. My dad always said that I was never happy with anything, and I should be, I should be happy with my lot in life, shouldn't I? I knew, KNEW that I had nothing to moan about, so why did I feel so empty, so trapped?

Urgh, looking back at my face, I started to apply the make-up, my armour against the world, my way of making me feel like I belonged in a world that I no longer knew my place in.

Right! I gave myself a stern look in the mirror and started waggling my finger in front of me. "Right, Kim, you've got a lot to be grateful for. You need to snap out of this right now!" Looking at the bottom of the mirror, I thought I saw something shimmering. Thinking it was just a bit of a mark, I reached out to clean it and watched as my hand disappeared through the mirror. I quickly snapped it back out and held the hand close to my chest. "What the hell just happened?" I mumbled to myself while shaking my head. I was tired, that had to be the reason. Okay, maybe I could use this time to sleep. Nodding to myself, happy that I was taking action, I turned around to walk back to my bed when I heard a voice call my name. Okay, where was that coming from? "John, is that you? Did you forget something?" Silence met my questions. Okay, so not John. I looked back in the mirror; this time, a hand came out and grabbed me and, before I knew what was happening, I was being dragged through the mirror.

I stretched up in bed, woken by a sound. "Where is that coming from?" I sat up in bed, feeling like I had slept for an age. *Ah a sleep is exactly what I needed*, I thought, as I swung my legs over the side of the bed and stood up. That was strange, no aches. I stretched, enjoying this new freedom of movement. "Wow, I really did need to sleep!"

I looked around my bedroom; everything looked the same, but it felt different. There was a lightness to the room, the sun shining its rays through the window.

There was that sound again. It sounded like humming. I made my way cautiously down the stairs and into the kitchen while holding my hand above my eyes to shield them from the glaring sun. I cursed myself for not grabbing my sunglasses on the way down.

Feeling slightly off kilter, I stumbled into a chair. Deciding to give up with moving for a bit, I sat down only to hear that same noise. Weirdly, it wasn't freaking me out. Instead, I breathed it in and rejoiced in the feeling of wholeness and contentment. *This is where I'm supposed to be*, I thought to myself. Closing my eyes and facing towards the warm sun rays flowing into the kitchen, I smiled. I couldn't remember a sunnier day. I spent what seemed like a few minutes but could have been hours breathing it all in and enjoying the stillness.

Just as I was about to nod off, I picked up a new

noise, my kids playing in the garden. As the noise got louder, I turned towards the double doors at the end of the kitchen. I could just about make out their outlines through the sun's rays as they ran, chasing each other outside. "So, they can play together nicely," I whispered to myself as I once again closed my eyes. A tickle of a memory started at the back of my mind. Weren't they out with John? I felt like there was something there, just out of my grasp and, like having a name on the tip of your tongue, I knew it, but I just couldn't bring it forward. Everything felt slowed down and it was like two parts of me were at war with one another. One part wanted to shout and scream that I should be worrying right now, that something wasn't right, and the other part of me just wanted to let it all go and enjoy this moment.

"Yes, you're just at the start and you will feel lots more inner wars, but that's okay, it's all part of the journey," whispered that voice again and my eyes shot open. There in front of me was a figure. She didn't look ghostly, but she did seem to be surrounded by a glowing light. I logically put it down to the intense sunshine we were having but that didn't feel quite right. As she started to walk towards me, I wondered why I didn't feel scared at all; instead, looking at her felt like coming home.

"Is it you that has been humming?" I asked.

"Yes," she responded. "I find myself doing it without thinking. I just love this sunshine, don't you?"

"Okaaaayy," I drawled. "Umm, I really don't know how you got into my house but my kids are outside and

I need you to go, I don't even know you." I went to stand up and force her to leave but her next words shocked me into falling back into my seat.

"This is my home and those are my children," she whispered, as though she realised it was going to be a tough pill to swallow.

"Umm, say what?" I asked, raising my eyebrows. "Look, I don't know who you are but you need to go… John… John, are you here? Can you come and help please?"

"He's not here at the moment. It was important that I just speak to you." She spoke softly again as she moved towards me.

"Right, you are really starting to…" I froze, unable to make a sound as she stepped in front of me, blocking out the sun, so I could see her clearly. She looked identical to me! I mean, she looked younger, fresher-faced, but the similarities were uncanny. "Uh, uh…" I couldn't form anything coherent at all.

"I know," she whispered. "I know this is very strange, but I had to see you."

"Who… are… you?" I stuttered, blinking my eyes in the hope that they would show me a different vision in front of me.

"I'm you." She smiled softly.

"But… that's not possible. I mean, am I hallucinating right now? No… no, I'm asleep." I started pinching my arm. "Come on, come on, wake up, this is too weird."

"I haven't got long," other me said, as she reached

out to take my arm and pull me up to standing "I'm you, just a different version, a future possibility. You're not supposed to be here right now but me coming to you wouldn't have been enough. You needed to see this for yourself."

"Okay, let's just say that I believe you. What do you want to show me?" I asked with my hand propped on my hip. I was so confused. I had gone from waking up feeling more rested than ever before to feeling completely out of my depth and convinced I was having some kind of breakdown.

She held my hand and led me to the open doors that opened to the garden. In front of me, the whole garden shimmered from my plain back garden into an oasis of nature. All around there were trees, bushes and flowers, birds flying from one to the other, and could I hear the sea? "Yes." She answered my thoughts for me. "We're near the sea. I didn't want to freak you out, so I made it look like our old home until it was time for you to see." I looked back into the kitchen to see a different kitchen too. It wasn't huge but it was spacious and cosy looking with an old cottage kitchen look. I looked back into the garden, taking it all in. I could still hear my children giggling and I instantly felt like I was home.

She turned to face me. "You think you feel trapped, powerless to what is happening around you. You feel that life is passing you by and yet you feel you are missing something, yes?" She looked straight at me, her stare unwavering.

I felt myself nodding slowly. "Yes, that about sums it up."

She continued to look directly into my soul as she said, "The power for change has always been and will always be inside you. Life happens FOR you, not TO you. Stop living according to other peoples' expectations and start living for you. Work out what you want from life and go after it." She glanced away before looking back at me and, taking a deep breath, she exhaled as she said, "You are NOT selfish to want more. The more you live a life of joy, the more you will inspire those around you to do the same and that thing you are missing" – she took a moment – "is the real you. You feel like something is missing because you're not being true to yourself. When you get back, work out who the real you is and then be her, every day, without apologies."

"Right, I've no idea how to do that," I mumbled. Was I actually starting to believe this?

"You don't have to start big. Start small, start asking yourself questions about what brings you joy, what lights you up – how can you do more of that each day?" She chuckled to herself. "The more you do this, the more it snowballs and you will find yourself making decisions and living new experiences you didn't think were even possible." She smiled while opening her arms to show the life that she was living.

She stood back. "Look at me. I was you and I didn't believe it was true, but it is. You just have to make the decision to start."

"To start? But how do I start?" But as I looked at her, she was already fading.

"Make the decision," she whispered before she completely disappeared.

I blinked, completely unsure whether to believe what I was seeing. As I opened my eyes, I jumped back. I was back in my bedroom, staring into the mirror with my make-up half done. "What the hell was that?" I questioned, looking at myself in the mirror. I looked different; even the side where I hadn't put my make-up on. I looked fresher. I couldn't believe it, I felt fresher too, like I'd been given a new life. As I went to turn away, I caught a sparkle in my eye that hadn't been there before, and I watched, mesmerised, as my reflection smiled and winked at me. I looked down at the cloth on the dressing table and started to wipe my make-up off. I was fed up of hiding, of trying to fit in. It was time to be the real me. Whatever that looked like, I had no idea, but it would be a fun journey finding out.

★★★

Kate lives in Leicestershire and is a mum of two. This is her first published work of fiction, although she is an avid reader. Kate is the owner of Kate Carter Coaching where she supports entrepreneurs and coaches to break the cycle of anxiety:

https://katecarter.co.uk/

A DAY IN THE LIFE OF AN OUTDOOR CAT

Lauren Raybould

Bright rays of the sun shone through the partially opened blind of the bedroom. I stretched all four of my legs and yawned. I heard four different patterns of breathing, which means they're all still asleep. That's fine.

They won't be asleep for much longer.

Licking the fur on my right leg a few times, I stood up and arched my back, stretching. Still, no one had stirred.

Alright, I thought. *Stage one commences.*

Turning to face the bed, I sat down, watching them sleep. After a few moments, I started meowing quietly at first, gradually getting louder. Akira's big ears twitched as he woke and turned to look at me. He too stretched out his legs, but then flopped his head back down and fell asleep again.

It's just me this morning, then.

The female human stirred, but it was only to move around. She's the one that needed to wake up, but if I wake all of them, then so be it.

Right, it's time to commence stage two. And she's not going to like this one – I've done it before, and it works every time.

I hopped onto the warm windowsill, right next to the spider plant there. Wasting no time, I started chewing only the very top leaves – not the ones coming out at the sides. It had to be the top ones.

Looking over to see her wake, I was right. She jerked away, looked at me, and hissed. I turned back and started nibbling again. No, I was determined that she wake up and feed me.

I heard her mutter, "It's 6am… no, Leo."

Ignoring her, I carried on with my quest to move this human. Expecting to hear the bed creak as she rose, I was surprised when I only heard the sheets moving. I stopped nibbling, and as I turned to face them again, a sock lightly slaps me in the face. Naturally, I jumped and ran out of the bedroom door. How dare she?! This worked all the time; I couldn't believe I was unsuccessful.

At the very least, Akira woke up this time, and he stretched as he got out of the bed, farting as he did so.

Ugh, that disgusting husky. At least, he will wake them by pacing, I thought. *He's finally joined in with waking them up.*

I crept back into the room to find Bella snoring softly, her brown paws twitching in her sleep. Akira was standing over the female human, attempting to lick her arm, which hung outside of the duvet. Now was my chance.

Commence stage three.

Gracefully (if I do say so myself), I pounced onto the bed, stepping on the sleeping male human, and onto the stomach of the sleeping female human. Digging my claws into the duvet (it feels nice, okay?), I meowed loudly in her face. She frowned, before opening her eyes and staring at me. I continued meowing; Akira howled, quieter than usual. Finally, we proved to be successful. Sighing, the human peeled back the duvet; I hopped off and, once again, stepping on the other human, I went out into the hallway to meow again. Akira followed, tail wagging, almost knocking me over in his excitement. Bella followed slowly, still half asleep.

Stupid dog. He's only getting fed thanks to me.

I waited on the third step from the top of the stairs for her, continually meowing, reminding her that I'm famished. Akira appeared by her side and bounded down the stairs. I scurried down quickly to avoid being squished by the big lump. He chased me into the kitchen, howling with happiness as he waited for food.

After I'm fed, I waited patiently on the second step to venture outside. The door opened, and I leaped out and under the fence into next door's garden. It was quite warm outside, so I laid down on the grass for a while. Though it was different today; outside was different. Normally, I watch the humans pass by, some walking dogs, others going to work or school. No, today was different. In the space of an hour, I saw one human walking past. This wasn't right at all.

I heard the door to my house open and watched as the human and the two dogs walked out. Akira spotted me and tried to pull on his lead. I darted off, bolting across the road and into the allotment. From there, I see the human take a left (my right) and begin their walk.

That's one normal thing, I thought. *I'd better avoid them; otherwise, Akira will want to chase me. And I can't be bothered to scratch him right now.*

A few houses away, I spotted the ginger and white cat I fought with last week, with his tabby cat sister. Up on my feet again, I prowled past their garden – strutted almost. He knew I was there, as I heard a low hiss, which I gladly returned. He leaped from his sunbathing spot and headed towards me. I turned back around, claws ready. He started growling, while his sister hissed, but stayed away. I yowled at him and pounced forward. Each time I yowled, I batted his head with my paw, but not hard enough to actually hurt him. The fights are fun, and yes, I dislike him, but I couldn't be bothered to have a proper scrap. He hopped back but was soon batting at my ear. I returned the sentiment, and just as he was going to do it again, his human came out and shouted at both of us, shooing me away.

This was the second human I'd seen today, not counting my human. There's usually more out and about. I saw their dog looking through the window at me. I took off down the street, past my house, and went in search of a shady spot. I ended up in a garden in the next street along; it's a usual spot of mine, where I like to hang out. These humans don't let their cat out, so it's amusing to see this tiny tabby cat watching me like a hawk in the window. Ha.

I stayed there for a while and watched as a few cars and a van drove by. Still, there weren't many humans. Actually, this was starting to get boring. No one had given me any attention, not even a glance. I started making my way back home, hoping to get let in, and I'll meow until I get belly rubs.

Satisfied with this plan, I strolled back onto my road, where I spotted a human walking past with a shopping bag. Then, I saw another human crossing the road and going into their house. These two were boring, though. I continued on my journey. I snuck under next door's fence and into their garden; from the sounds of it, my human and those wretched dogs had already returned and were in the back garden, sprawled across the grass.

As I reached the front door, the female human opened it. But I didn't feel like going in, so I stayed put, looking up at her. Akira appeared at her side, his tail wagging. Yeah, I'm definitely not going in.

The human sighed and made a *pspspsps* sound – a rather weak attempt at enticing me in. I stayed put and stared.

Akira barked at me, so I leapt on the dustbin and stared from a distance. The human stopped him from leaving the house. I started to walk away from the door, so she shut it. That's fine with me.

After a few minutes of lying down in our garden, I went back to the door and meowed. It took her a few minutes, but she opened the door again, and I could tell she wasn't impressed. She didn't like the door games I played with her, but they're fun – for me anyway.

I strolled into the hallway and up a few of the steps before Bella barked (stopping when she noticed it was me and walked back to her bed), but Akira chased me upstairs, where I hissed at him from the high windowsill. He sniffed me, licked my ears and head, before he bowed and jumped up, expecting me to play.

He always looks so happy, I thought. Well, if we must play, I can at least make this fun for me.

So, I hissed and pretended to bat him with my paw. He dodged and barked at me, egging me on.

He's getting brave. Maybe it's time to teach him a little lesson.

Jumping onto the carpet, I spooked him by chasing *him* down the stairs and into the living room, though it's all a game to him. As Bella stared from the comfort of her bed, I leapt up onto the safety of the armchair, while Akira bowed and barked at me to play again. Seriously, there was no deterring him. You've got to hand it to him – he's persistent, but it's annoying and tedious. I tired of playing with him quickly, so I lay down and ignored him. The human eventually told him to be quiet, which was amusing. He obeyed like the good boy he is.

The human walked out of the room, so I followed her into the kitchen. She pottered about, and so I meowed at her to get her attention. She gave in and stroked me, before fetching some fishy treats from the cupboard for me. Gobbling them down and now satisfied with the attention I'd received, I headed to the front door and started meowing again.

Being let out again, I headed to the other neighbour's house, where I ignored their barking dog in the window as this human, wearing a mask and gloves, fed me some chicken treats as he left his house. With one last stroke of my head, he climbed into his car and drove off.

This really is such a boring day.

I meandered around the streets for a bit, seeing if there were any other cats around, but most were inside. There was a white cat with brown spots, who dashed out of his garden to bat at an unlucky squirrel, who quickly scampered up a tree. The cat paused, deliberated on whether to follow it up the tree, then skulked off back to their garden.

I found a big car to sit under for a bit when I spotted my female human coming out of the house by herself; Akira watched from the window as she left. I decided to follow her. Instantly, she spotted me, smiled, and stroked me before continuing on her way. I followed her down the hill, spotting the other black and grey cat in his garden as we passed. I stared at him as I walked past. He stared back, one leg stretched up in the air as he licked his fur. We turned a corner, and she gave me more fuss before disappearing into the shop. She did this sometimes, and she never gets me any treats. I sat by the door, staring into the shop and watching her. The shop's grey cat rounded the corner, spotted me and ran off, so I attempted to eat some of the kibble left out for her. It was awful, but I ate some anyway. The human spotted this and said, "Oi, Leo." So, I stopped and stared at her before following her back home.

We passed that black and grey cat again – I can't remember his name. He was closer to the fence now and approached me as I walked past. The human stopped to pet him, but I wasn't having that, so I walked up to him. I hissed and batted at him. He pawed at me back, claws out, but the human got in the way and separated us. She didn't look happy with me.

We reached home, and I went in straight away this time. It's always good to keep them guessing. As usual, Akira chased me but soon turned his attention to the human in the kitchen. I went upstairs to see the male human, who sat at his desk. He turned to fuss me and scratch my back – that felt so nice. Finally, I had some decent fuss, considering the lack of humans outside today. I heard the clanking of bowls downstairs and dashed down to get my dinner.

Once again, I went back out for a wander, just in case other humans were walking around. There was no one. One car passed me, but that was it. I skulked into my back garden, where Akira was in the corner, chasing a pigeon away. He didn't spot me. I looked into the back door, where both humans were. They started calling my name, but I walked off, not looking back.

Moments later, I appeared at the front door, meowing to come in. Once again, they obliged, and the male human opened the door.

As I settled down for the evening, I strolled into the bedroom, where the female sat in bed on her laptop. Bella was at the bottom of the bed, but Akira was by the human's side, curled up (yet, somehow, he still took up most of the bed).

Tentatively, I stepped onto the bed but paused. Akira lifted his head and looked at me with sleepy eyes but soon fell asleep again. I resumed walking up to the human and leapt onto her lap, where her laptop was. Plonking myself down partially on the keyboard, I rolled onto my back and purred. No one could resist this. It was the ultimate plan for fuss. And alas, it worked.

Setting aside her laptop, she began to rub my belly and my head. My purring intensified, and I was in heaven. After a while, I'd had enough and got up in search of my own bed near the windowsill. I settled down there for the night, wondering if I would maybe wake the humans earlier tomorrow. And hopefully, there were more humans giving me fuss outside.

***

From Leicester, Lauren is a freelance journalist and editor who is the owner of The Night Owl Editing, and provides editing, proofreading and copywriting services to businesses and individuals. When not working, she's either reading a book, walking her dogs or going to music gigs and blogging about them.

THE CONVENT

Sarah Carter

I don't remember my first memory of being there. I just always was. There was no one there to tell me when I said my first word, or what that first word was. Everyone has their lists of firsts, right? Parents and families, to show them pictures and tales of when they were little. Nope, not me. I wasn't even sure of when my birthday was. They told me it was the 29th October, but I think that may have been made up. It was probably the first day I had arrived, or something, as a two-year-old girl being carried in a basket on the front of a policeman's bicycle. Or so I was told that's how I came to be here. I was an orphan, you see. Although I did have a mother. She would come and visit sometimes. But I was never quite sure why it was that my mother handed me over, to be raised by nuns in a convent. I'm sure she was doing the best she could; I like to think so. I'm sure that she thought that I would be looked after and cared for by the nuns when, perhaps, she could not do this herself. I don't know. I like to look on the brighter side of things.

All I knew was life was tough living in a convent.

You really were just surviving, day by day when you are treated just as a number, and as a huge inconvenience. But, despite all of this, there was still fun and adventure to be found.

For some reason, I couldn't sleep. I was thinking about Mum and wondering when I would see her again. It had been weeks now. It felt like years.

It was a windy night and the wind was howling like a ghost as it blew through the gaps in the windows. My bed was next to the window, which was good when the sunshine shone through and touched your face in the morning to gently wake you up. But it was cold and dark, and the cold draft whispered through the room, making my skin goosepimply. I pulled the blanket over my face and covered my nose and panted heavily, so it would warm the blanket. I was trying to savour every warm breath I had, drawing each breath out until my lungs were completely empty.

I was trying my hardest to distract my mind from the fact that I really needed a wee. I was going to have to wait until the morning. We weren't allowed to get up in the night, it was against the rules. Even if we had to use the toilet. But if I didn't go, I was sure to wet the bed, and the other girls would find out and laugh at me. I thought about every possibility of what I could do to avoid me getting up and walking down the hallway to the toilet. I even thought whether it would be possible to wee in the gaps of the floorboards by my bed, or I could wee by the window and say that it rained last night and that the window leaked. I jiggled so much that my metal-framed bed started to shake and nudge across the floor.

"Nelly, is that you?" A soft and delicate voice cut through the darkness. It was my friend Toddy, who slept in the bed opposite to me. "What's wrong?" Toddy called.

"I need a wee, Toddy," I said. "I'm so desperate I'm going to pee myself."

"Just go, will you. You're going to wake everyone up. She'll definitely hear you if you carry on like this. Just go quietly and I'll snore loudly so she doesn't hear the floorboards."

She's right, I had to do it. "Okay, I'm going," I called. I slowly uncovered my legs and put my bare feet onto the wooden floorboards, slowly lifting my body up with my arms and gradually, very slowly putting my weight onto my legs. I stood up. I was going to have to be quick if I was going to make it to the toilet without wetting myself. I crept, creeping like a lizard, hunched over with my arms out to balance me, trying to soften every step. My body was so tense, and I couldn't see a thing; it was pitch black.

I was nearly there. Toddy's snores were comforting to listen to as I slowly stepped my way to the loo, my arms stretched out, feeling the way. With my hands lowered, I could feel the toilet, then with a swizzle, I backed myself up to the seat. It was freezing, but I didn't care. I was so desperate for a wee, it was just a huge relief to have made it. I started to relax as I went for what seemed like the longest wee ever. But then, I heard a door go. Heavy footsteps stomped across the room, heading towards me. It was her. It was definitely her. I had a sudden pang of dread as my heart sank deep within my stomach. I started being able to see more. Her door must be open, spreading the light from her lamp across the darkened room. Then a shadow stood in the doorframe, tall and wide. "Nelly Flynn. I should have known it was you out of bed. What are you doing out of your bed at this hour, how dare you?" I barely had time to pull my knickers back up before she yanked me by my skinny arm and marched me into her room. She threw me into a large wooden chair that stood by a small table at the bottom of her bed.

"Stay there, you wretched little animal," she sneered. "Are you not aware of the rules, girl? You are not allowed to move from your bed during lights out. And what's more, I heard you making a noise, a noise that would make the virgin Mary blush. So, that's five lashings for you." (It was also forbidden to make a tinkling sound when you went to the toilet.) She stood over me waving her trotter-like fingers at me as she barked in her deep and gruff voice. I sat in the chair, leaning back trying to gain some space between my face and her hand, as she was waving it around while she yelled. When she had finished, I looked up. Daring to look the beast in the eye. And she really was a beast. Her breath was vile, like she'd been on a faeces-only diet all her life.

"I'm, I'm sorry miss," I stuttered. "I was just so desperate I thought I was going to wet the bed."

"Well you should have gone before lights out, shouldn't you? You'll get no sympathy, silly child." She reached out to get her cane from underneath her pillow. "Hold your hands out, Nelly, you know the drill."

I knew the drill. This was not the first time I'd had the displeasure of getting lashings from Mrs Thornton. She gave them out liberally. I wished she would just get it over with. The suspense was almost as bad as getting them. I held my hands out and closed my eyes, waiting for the cane to get smacked across my knuckles. Whack. The first one hit. I could hear the whistle as it built up momentum flying through the air. It stung, but I must not make a noise. It would anger her even more. My teeth gritted, trying to keep my screams in, I tried to focus on the candle flickering in the corner of the room, thinking of anything but what was happening.

"Keep still, you wretched child," she hissed. "Number four," she counted as she slammed down another blow. I looked at my hands, now bright red. Even in the dimmed light of the oil lamp, I could see it. The pain was so bad it felt as if they should be pumping out blood. I couldn't stop my hands from shaking. "Right, five more for you as you're not keeping still. This will teach you to move while I'm trying to teach you a lesson. Ungrateful little brat." Each slam felt like it was breaking my bones. I wished my fingers would just drop off; maybe then they'd stop hurting so much.

I had ten lashings in total and was told to go straight back to sleep. I got into bed. I didn't feel the cold anymore. At least that was something. At least the lashings on my knuckles gave me some warmth. They were burning hot.

"Psst, you okay, Nelly?" Toddy whispered. "I'm sorry, I tried to snore as loud as I could."

"Don't worry," I whispered back. "At least I didn't wet the bed."

I couldn't sleep then. My hands were throbbing too much. I lay in bed thinking of all the ways that I could escape this place and go and find my mum. But I had no idea where she lived.

Just then, in the corner of my eye, I saw a light coming into the convent driveway. Then the devil woman, Mrs Thornton, came rushing out of her room, putting on her black coat as she walked down the stairs.

"Toddy, psst," I called. "Are you still awake?"

I waited with my ears wide open. I was listening so hard, I'm pretty sure that I could hear a spider spinning her web in the corner of the room.

I could hear a girl screaming. I looked out of the window to see if I could see anything, but I couldn't. I've never heard anyone squeal like it. It was like she was being tortured or something. The other girls in the room started to wake. "What was that?" a voice called out of the darkness. "What's going on?" One by one, I could see in the shadows the girls' heads pop up. The noise was so loud. I heard them coming up the stairs and the door slamming. The girl wasn't even stopping to take a breath. It was just a constant squeal. The lights began to go back down the driveway towards the road. It must have been Jim, the policeman. He often brought babies and girls to the convent. The smaller ones arrived in a basket on the front of his bicycle. He was a nice man and would often come to see us children and play games with us on the lawn in the summertime. Once, we did the conga, about thirty children lined up behind him, and we went around the whole convent singing. It was one of my best days.

This was not a good day. I heard them getting closer.

"What's happening?" Toddy said, jumping into my bed with me. We ducked under the covers. The other girls were darting all around the room too. It was chaos and if Mrs Thornton caught us, it would be mass lashings all around for sure.

"It's a girl," I said.

"It sounds like a wild animal," said Toddy. The screams were getting louder and closer. Then I heard a sharp bang, like a massive stamp on the wooden stairs. Then, the screaming stopped. I assumed that was her, the devil woman, giving her a piece of her mind. Showing her who was boss around here. It all went deadly silent for a few seconds and everyone was waiting and listening. Then the footsteps started again and the girls that had got out of bed to take a look rushed back to their own beds. Toddy ran back too. Maybe she's killed her, I thought. I wouldn't put it past her.

They were in the room now and walked right past the bottom of my bed. It was a girl. I could just about make her out in the shadows with my eyes squinting. She was panting, probably from all that screaming. I'm surprised she didn't pass out from the lack of oxygen. Girls often joined us here but never normally in the middle of the night. I wondered what must have happened to her. "Now be quiet and get some sleep," she was told by Mrs Thornton, as she marched back off to her room leaving the girl laying on top of her bed. I could see the light shining from the gap underneath Governess's door. A few moments passed and the light went out, leaving us in the darkness.

"Hey you," I whispered. "You okay?"

Nothing came back. "Oi you, can you hear me?"

"Just leave me alone," a voice said back. I wasn't sure what to say to her. I wanted to help her, comfort her as I knew how it felt. My heart felt heavy and sad for her. I could hear the pain, feel it. It was so strong it radiated.

"You have a really impressive scream," I said. It was the only thing I could think of to say to her.

"Thanks," she said back.

Morning finally came. I was awake. It was the crack of dawn. The darkness remained in the room but the daylight was slowly softening it. I could just about make out the rows of beds where the other girls were sleeping. There were around ten beds to a dormitory. All was still, and all was quiet, with just the soft sounds of the girls' sleepy breaths whistling in and out of their mouths. I heard the cockerel crow from a distant farm. I'd been listening for a while now, to her, the witch of a woman clattering around in her room whilst she got herself ready for the day. Her room was at the bottom of the dormitory. Then I heard her stepping on the creaky floorboards as she walked towards her door. As soon as I heard them squeak, my tummy filled with dread. A kind of sinking ship feeling in your body, as your soul sinks towards your toes and tries to escape out of your toenails. She tried to suck the soul out of every single one of us, I'm sure of it.

"Up, girls!" she yelled, as she rang the bell. "Get dressed, you have ten minutes." My moments of dreaming were over, and it was time to begin the day.

I got up and got dressed as I did every day. I knew the drill and knew that the day ahead was going to be tough. But, despite this, I felt excited. There was lots to be positive about. There was the new girl to get to know and I always believed that something wonderful was about to happen. You never do know what's around the corner. I just hoped it would be something great.

★★★

Sarah Carter lives in Leicestershire with her husband and two children, as well as their three spaniels, Bella, Lola and Luna. She has been a florist for seventeen years and grows flowers in her garden to work with for weddings and events:

www.sarahcarterflowers@gmail.com

MASTERPIECES

Michelle Chambers

★ Warning: this story contains graphic descriptions of crime scenes that some readers may find disturbing ★

Gabby finally calmed her nightmares enough to get some sleep. After working a gruesome case all week with no leads, it was really eating at her. As soon as she drifted into a deep sleep her phone rang. Groggy, she slapped her hand around the nightstand until it landed on her phone.

She answered abruptly, 'DCI Brewyn.'

'Guv, we have another one.'

'Where?'

'In Queen Elizabeth Park.'

'Okay, I'll be there in twenty.'

Gabby sluggishly got out of bed to find the pale grey suit and slightly stained shirt she had only just got out of hours earlier to put them back on again. This was the third case like this this week, meaning there was a serial killer out there, which was way beyond what Gabby was prepared to deal with. Up until now, she had only dealt with open and shut cases, a few murders but those were mainly drug or domestic related, none of which equipped her for a sadistic serial killer. She purposely came to England for university to pursue a career in law enforcement because she believed the lack of guns meant a lack of crimes. Gabby didn't realise that there are sickos everywhere, not just in the States, not just in Chicago and now in the quaint English countryside.

She had only been promoted to chief inspector a month earlier and that made her the youngest female in the Criminal Investigations Department to ever hold a DCI rank in the UK. Not only was she facing discrimination amongst the men she worked with for being their boss but the fact she was American didn't go down so well either. Despite being in England for over ten years, people assumed she was fresh from the airport and had no knowledge of English law; even though she graduated with a first from the University of Surrey, arguably the best university to study criminology in the UK.

When she arrived at the scene just after 3am, there was already the faintest hint of dawn on the horizon. Forensics were at work trying to find any physical evidence to give them a suspect. The previous two cases left nothing, no hair, no fingerprints, no DNA. With the bodies being left out in the elements, it was even more difficult to get anything from them. The previous two victims had their fingertips and toes burned off, as well as all their teeth pulled from their mouth. So not only did they have no suspects, they also had no idea who their victims were.

Although Gabby felt awful not knowing who these people were, she was also slightly relieved that she didn't have to tell the family members the horrendous details of the brutality and torture they'd been through. From the evidence they did have, it was clear that they had been systematically tortured and more than likely held captive for days if not weeks before they were eventually killed and disposed of.

As an empath, Gabby truly felt every emotional and physical wound of those around her, including her cases. It was the main reason why she hadn't been with anyone since she graduated. It wasn't because she's not attractive, although as of late she had been taking less care of herself, but to carry that into a relationship is hard. As soon as Gabby saw the decapitated head with a rat in the victim's toothless mouth, her whole body constricted as she envisioned her own mouth pried open with a dead maggot-infested rodent.

Gabby walked across the dew-covered grass to locate all of the body parts that had been scattered throughout Queen Elizabeth Park. Everything about this was planned to the nth degree. There was no mistaking that there was more of this to come and the killer was sending a message, but what? The victim's head was found near the north entrance of the park. The grass had been cleared around it, and for the brutality of this crime the killer took such care and precision placing the body, setting the scene for the story they were trying to tell us.

'GUV! Quick!'

Gabby ran to where she heard DS Jordan shouting. As she approached the middle of the park with the moss-strewn Victorian fountain, she could see that blood had now replaced the water that had been there. The blood was bubbling and frothing as it poured from the spouts. As Gabby and the other officers stood aghast, taking in everything, they saw the victim's heart elegantly placed in the baby angel's hands that adorned the top of the fountain. This was new, this was the first time any of the organs had been removed. The other two victims, known simply as Jane and John Doe, had all their organs intact and all of their extremities where found. If this was a sign of the killer escalating, Gabby dared not to think what would be coming next.

Forensics started to take photos and samples of the blood to hopefully get a hit for DNA, although doubtful. From what evidence was gathered about the other two victims, both were between twenty-five and forty, Caucasian, no identifiable marks, nothing to actually help find out who these people were. This led Gabby to believe that they definitely weren't in the system; as the killer went to such lengths to hide their identity, they would have researched if their victim had ever been incarcerated.

Gabby had sent DS Jordan to check out the east side of the park, DS O'Shea to check the west and she would check the south. She stressed the importance of finding the rest of the body as soon as possible. This wasn't only to preserve as much evidence as they could but also to clear the park quickly before people started waking up. The CI Department had kept a closed lid on the previous two cases, as they didn't want to scare the public, especially as they had nothing to give them. Everyone had been sworn to secrecy and the press would only be contacted for a press conference from the Chief Constable. Gabby knew that a press conference would now be imminent as this was the third body in a week, the killer had escalated in the mutilation of the body and the white marbled fountain had already begun to stain with blood; there was no hiding this one.

The lights in the park had switched off as dawn broke in the midlands. Sniffer dogs had been sent out across the park to assist in finding the rest of the body and all Gabby could hear was constant barking. She was anxious to find the torso and lower half of the victim's body to at least determine their gender. Jane and John Doe had been placed in a deserted industrial estate and near the moors of the Peak District. Although the areas were sparse, the body parts were laid quite close together and were placed in a way that resembled a body. This being the case, it was only right for Gabby to assume with the head on the north side, the heart in the middle, that the torso and legs would be found near the south.

She was away with her thoughts about the previous cases when she found a pair of breasts stuck to a tree trunk. Gabby instinctively shrieked and hugged her own for reassurance that they were still there. She now knew that the third victim was Jane Doe II. The killer kept Jane Doe's breasts on the body, so why take them off for this one? Gabby called forensics to her location over the radio as she took a closer look at the breasts. She could tell that the breasts had had implants, but where were they? Anything that goes into the body has to have serial numbers to identify the pieces used and are registered to the person that is using them. Gabby had hoped there would be some sign of the implants left, but nothing.

The killer must have known Jane Doe II, it was vicious and ruthless, and she had been put in a public place, almost on display. Gabby thought that the killer could have possibly wanted the publicity so put her in a public place, or it could be something much deeper, darker and more sadistic than even the most seasoned investigators had come across.

She had put on her gloves to further inspect the mutilated breasts, the cuts and removal was expertly done, so potentially a doctor, a coroner, a butcher, someone trained with a knife. Again, Gabby's mind raced as she thought about how gracefully everything was done. She shuddered for thinking something so horrendous could be graceful, but it was. This person was a storyteller, they were on a mission; whether it was a long story or each victim had an individual story of their own, there was a rhyme and reason for all of this. The killer definitely wanted them to pay attention to the minor details, the care they had put into all of this. As she was taking in the scene, she noticed something odd about the right breast: she had an inverted nipple! Now, this wouldn't normally be something of great importance, but in this instance, it could lead to some idea as to who she was. Only people who knew her intimately would know that she had implants and an inverted nipple. Gabby also had an inverted nipple and knew that about ten percent of women have it, but it can be corrected by augmentation. Maybe this is why Jane Doe II wanted implants, but the nipple was unsuccessful.

When forensics got to where Gabby was, DS Jordan and O'Shea were there as well. They told Gabby how they had found the left and right arm right by the east and west entrances, identical in placement, and how they were cut just around the shoulder and like the others her fingerprints had been burnt off. Gabby got them up to speed with what she knew about the breasts when DS Jordan interrupted: 'Ha, you sure know a lot about boobs!'

Gabby sent a scornful look and said, 'Well, unlike you, I've seen more than just my mom's boobs, so unless you have anything else funny to say about this poor woman, I suggest you start looking for her torso, as I'm sure the sight of her vagina will send you into a giggle fit.'

DS O'Shea snickered under his breath and DS Jordan went bright red as he strode off with a few other officers looking for the torso. Gabby was always dealing with snide comments and jokes and she usually brushed them off, but even for Gabby that was just in poor taste.

If the arms were located to the east and west, she was right in her theory of the parts being spread out over the park as they are placed on the body. So, with DS Jordan looking for a torso, she went straight to the south entrance where she was certain she was going to find the lower half of Jane Doe II's body. Gabby was almost at the south entrance when she heard DS Jordan shout for forensics, so she knew that he had found what he was looking for. All that was left was her lower half, hopefully in one piece.

In the distance, Gabby saw the entrance gate and started to sprint towards it. Directly underneath the gate lay a pair of legs cut above the pubic bone. Her legs were open at a ninety-degree angle. There was bruising all over her thighs that looked a few days old and her toes had been burnt on the bottom. Gabby called the team to the south entrance as she scoured the scene for any other evidence, particularly asking why Jane Doe II's legs were wide open. As she was looking all over, the glare of the sun hitting the gate made Gabby look up. It had said, 'Thank you for visiting'. She then walked through the gate to see 'Everyone Welcome' on the front. The other two crimes didn't show any signs of sexual assault, but the implications for this murder were definitely going down that route. Gabby had put a police barricade around the perimeter of the park to stop anyone coming through as they normally did for early morning runs and dog walks.

Gabby knew now was the time to call a press conference before the locals saw anything and started spreading rumours. She pulled out her phone and got ready to call Chief Constable Davis to get the go ahead for the conference but, as she did, her phone rang. It was her superintendent.

'What the hell, Brewyn? Didn't we say that we needed Davis' approval before any press releases?!'

Confused, Gabby said, 'Yes, I was just about to call him, what is going on?'

'What's going on? I just got a call from the local BBC wondering if we'd like to release a statement on the latest murder in Queen Elizabeth Park!'

'What do you mean? How do they know? We are still working the scene, no one has been in or out since I arrived at three.'

'Well, someone has tipped off the press, so be prepared, and don't say anything! Just tell them that we will be releasing a statement later.'

'Okay, I understand.'

When Gabby got off the phone, she was bemused at the thought of someone tipping off the press. Surely no one would want that right now? Maybe DS Jordan to get back at Gabby for her calling him out, but no, he wouldn't risk his job just for that. She was just about to call the team to update them about the press coming and to not say anything when her phone rang again. This time it was from an unknown number, and she suspected it was the press already working their way down the ranks to see who would talk.

'DCI Brewyn.'

'Oh, hello, DCI Brewyn. So formal, do you mind if I call you Gabby?'

'Um, who is this?'

'You're sweet, don't be coy, you've been expecting my call.'

'If this is the BBC, I'm sorry but we will formally release a statement later.'

'Oh, Gabby, I'm not the BBC, I'm the one who phoned them.'

Gabby's knees wobbled and she had to grab onto a nearby tree to balance herself. Could this be the killer? How did they get my number? They had an odd voice and it was hard to tell if they were male or female. Gabby tried to get DS O'Shea's attention to start tracing the call but before she could tell him she heard them say, 'Don't bother trying to trace this call, it will just be a lot of needless work, as you'll never find where I am.'

Gabby was frozen. She said, 'Are you the person responsible for this murder?'

'Murder? Oh, no honey, I'm responsible for the artwork, I just use different paints than most.'

Taken aback, Gabby knew she had to keep them talking to find out as much as she could about them.

'Oh? This is your idea of art, then what were your other two pieces?'

'That was for starters, to make sure you were paying attention for my masterpieces.'

'Well, it's truly something, I'd love to pay my respects to the artist.'

'There will be a time for that, but I really must get started on my next piece.'

'I thought you said you wanted me to pay attention to your masterpieces?'

'I did, but it wasn't a play on words, although I think I like that, the master of pieces, hmm, it can be a working name. I have more work to get to, I look forward to talking to you more, but I think the press should be there shortly, so you'll need to get ready.'

What was that? Gabby thought she was playing a part in a Dean Koontz novel, surely this doesn't happen in real life, what is going on? She started to hyperventilate as DS O'Shea came over to find out what just happened. She told him everything that had just transpired and wanted them to try and triangulate the call to see if they could get anything from it. Just then DS Jordan ran up to Gabby and said, 'They're here.'

Gabby pushes her way past the police barricade to find not only the BBC but multiple news agents and journalists, not to mention all of the town people trying to find out what was going on. At least fifteen people were shouting for her attention. Her eyes started to blur, her heart was pounding and her palms sweaty, what was she going to say?

A very authoritative voice rose above the rest. It was Robin Keyes from BBC News and she said, 'DCI Brewyn, we were alerted to a horrific crime that took place here this morning, can you tell us anything about that?'

'The department will be releasing an official statement on the matter later today.'

'What about the other two murders? Do you believe that they are linked?'

Gabby felt as though the wind got knocked out of her, the killer must have told them about the others.

'At this time, we are not prepared to give any details of open cases.'

'What about the phone call you just took, was it the killer? They said they would be calling you to see if you liked their art. Was there anything significant about the bodies that would help identify them?'

Stunned, all Gabby could say was, 'The killer cuts the bodies into pieces, and wants us all to see their masterpieces, and this is just the beginning.'

★★★

Michelle is a two-time best-selling author of non-fiction books and this is her first fiction contribution. She is originally from Chicago and met her husband whilst getting her Masters' Degree. She has two kids, a dog and is enjoying living in the East Midlands. She is a Mindset Coach and Mentor and has her own business The Best You:

www.thebestyouinstruction.com

If you've enjoyed reading this then please do leave a review on the Amazon page; it will make the authors do a happy dance!

If you're interested in being part of the next collection of short stories then please get in touch with Jen Parker:
contact@fuzzyflamingo.co.uk

For more information about publishing services, have a look at the website:
www.fuzzyflamingo.co.uk

Printed in Great Britain
by Amazon